Alaska Shelter

Debbie LaFleiche

Enjoy the journey!

Debbie LaFleiche

A Wings ePress, Inc.
Romance Suspense Novel

Wings ePress, Inc.

Edited by: Jeanne Smith
Copy Edited by: Christie Kraemer
Executive Editor: Jeanne Smith
Cover Artist: Trisha FitzGerald-Jung
Woman image from Ali Pazani at Pixels
Cabin image from Despotiphotos

All rights reserved

Names, characters and incidents depicted in this book are products of the author's imagination or are used fictitiously. Any resemblance to actual events, locales, organizations, or persons, living or dead, is entirely coincidental and beyond the intent of the author or the publisher.

No part of this book may be reproduced or transmitted in any form or by any means, electronic or mechanical, including photocopying, recording, or by any information storage and retrieval system, without permission in writing from the publisher.

Wings ePress Books
www.wingsepress.com

Copyright © 2022 by: Debbie LaFleiche
ISBN-13: 978-1-61309-512-6
ISBN-10: 1-61309-512-0

Published In the United States Of America

Wings ePress Inc.
3000 N. Rock Road
Newton, KS 67114

What They Are Saying About *Alaska Shelter*

From the very first page, I was immersed in this creative mystery. Debbie writes in an engaging and fun style that leads the reader on to the next page and the next as the protagonists seek to unravel a puzzle. I have to admit, I didn't guess the ending! An enjoyable read.
 —Lynda Rozell, author, *Journeys with a Tin Can Pilgrim: from corporate lawyer to Airstream nomad: finding joy in everyday life*

Author Debbie LaFleiche has written a page-turner that creates warmth despite its setting in the cold Alaskan temps. For anyone who loves romance and suspense in a gorgeous setting.
 —Lizbeth Meredith, author, *Pieces of Me: Rescuing My Kidnapped Daughters*, now a Lifetime original movie as *Stolen Hearts*

Debbie LaFleiche's debut novel, *Alaska Shelter,* is a fun, fast-paced romantic suspense that is sure to warm every reader's heart. Annabeth is a new accountant at Rescued Paws but Cooper, her boss, who has just returned from personal leave, meets her for the first time when he finds her in the office hallways after hours, threatened at gunpoint by a stranger. That is the beginning of Annabeth's and Cooper's race for time to uncover a scheme that eludes the Alaska police and threatens both their lives. Together they must piece together the clues of the stranger's cryptic demands, even as they are both nursing recent heartbreaks and still finding their footing as newly-single Alaskans. At the heart of it all is an adorable black lab puppy named Solstice who steals Annabeth's heart with her slobbering puppy kisses, and adds terminal cuteness to this engaging and heart-warming story. With *Alaska Shelter*, Debbie LaFleiche has established herself

as a skillful writer who can easily move from breathless tension to touching emotional revelation, making this novel a memorable start to a brilliant new series.
   —Laura Valeri, author, *After Life as a Human, Safe in Your Head, The Dead Still Here* and L'isola del Silenzio

Dedication

For Karen

* * *

One

Malcolm Cooper walked down the dark hallway toward the lobby of Rescued Paws, the place he loved and had worked for the last eight years. He had arrived that morning two hours before everyone else, even parking a couple blocks away, kept his office door closed all day and, when he finally emerged, it was two hours after closing. Good thing his office came with its own restroom, tiny as it was, he thought.

He just wasn't quite ready to face people. None of his staff even knew he'd returned from his eight weeks of extended leave. He'd meant to email them last week to let them know of his intent to return tomorrow, Wednesday. But he'd forgotten. Then, late last night, after Uber dropped him off at home from the airport, he decided a quiet day in the office, getting a handle on all he'd missed, might help keep his mind off of the reason he had taken the leave in the first place.

At the end of the hallway, he saw the weird shadows that played around the lobby when all but the overnight safety lights were off. He didn't bother turning on any others. There was enough of a glow to see by for his quick and final task of the day—dropping off the binder filled with eight weeks' worth of signed adoption certificates on the desk of Shannon, the office manager. Of course, he had hardly put a dent in the volume of work that had built up, but he felt accomplished at just having started. Eight weeks was a long time to be gone when you were the director of a small nonprofit organization.

Cooper yawned. His eyes blurred, then cleared. Food and sleep, nothing had sounded so good in a long time. At least the 14-hour work day had kept his not-yet-60-year-old mothers' death pushed to the back of his mind. But with the long work day coming to a close, it crept back in. Cooper's legs felt heavy as tree trunks and thoughts of the rapid-moving cancer that ravaged, and then took, his mother, suddenly overwhelmed him. The raw primal pain was back full force. No one should have to experience the pain of losing a parent and, yet, he knew, almost everyone would.

Just before he got to the end of hall that would open into the lobby, Cooper heard the whimper of a dog. He grew irritated, despite his adoration of them. He didn't have it in him tonight to corral the dog and return it to its kennel. Which employee forgot to secure a kennel, he wondered. Probably Simon, the facility manager. It wouldn't be the first time. Either he or one of the volunteers.

When he turned the corner, instead of a roaming dog, what he saw hit him with the force of a physical blow to the gut. Adrenaline shot through his veins. Fatigue gone. Grief gone. Hunger gone. Cooper took two steps back into the hallway to hide from view. That was no dog whimpering.

For a nanosecond, he didn't care about the work he got done in the last 14 hours. He wished to go back to this morning and not come into work. He should've stayed in bed, especially after that long flight back to Alaska yesterday from Florida. Since he was wishing, really, he wished he could go back eight weeks and have his mother not die. Further, even, to a year ago when the other death had occurred.

But that wasn't an option. Nor was it an option to ignore what he had just seen in the lobby. Tired or not, grieving or not, it just wasn't who he was.

Cooper peered around the corner to the middle of the lobby. He tried to take in the full scene before pulling back again.

It was a young woman, hands up in the "I surrender" position, a tall lanky man wearing a black stocking cap, his back to Cooper but angled in such a way that Cooper understood the woman's hands were raised because of the gun in his gloved hand. Who were these people and where did they come from?

"Tell me," Cooper heard the man say.

If the woman spoke, Cooper didn't hear it.

"Tell me," the man said louder, but in a low rough voice. "Or I'm going to hurt you."

Barely above a whisper, Cooper heard her reply. "I don't know." That had been the whimpering he'd heard.

What was going on? Cooper didn't recognize either of them. He didn't have a good position to see the man's face, but he didn't think he knew someone that tall and thin. Or with the longish, bushy brown hair poking out from the winter cap.

Cooper dared another look around the corner. "I'm not going to ask again." The man pointed the gun more forcefully at her, waggling it as if to make sure she saw it.

The woman jumped. "I told you I don't know what you're talking about. I would tell you if I knew."

Cooper could easily see the man's agitation increasing and ran through his options. No matter who these people were or why this was happening, he couldn't let the man shoot the defenseless woman. There was no way to call 911 without going back to his office, and he didn't dare leave the scene he'd stumbled into.

He looked around for something to use as a weapon, but he was in a hallway. Plaques and framed photos lined the walls. Nothing else. As the person who had hung them, he knew they were secure, and attempting to remove one silently would prove impossible. Though the large United Way plaque would be heavy enough to knock the gun out of the guy's hand. Why couldn't Paws have a coat rack nearby?

But, no, there was nothing. Cooper's mind raced. What to do?

If he could get to where they stood without the gunman noticing, the element of surprise could be to his advantage. It was probably the only advantage he'd have. It wasn't a weapon, but it was something. It was a terrible plan. And he knew he needed to do it anyway.

Cooper sucked in his breath, stepped out of the hallway again and into the lobby.

"I'm going to count to three," the gunman said. "Then things are going to get really real around here. Do you understand me?"

She didn't move. The woman lowered an arm to wipe her nose with the sleeve of her turtle neck sweater. As she returned her arm to the air, she looked up and caught sight of Cooper for the first time. Her eyes—bright blue, he could see even from this distance—grew to the size of poker chips.

Cooper put his finger to his lips, desperately hoping she wouldn't give him away because a gun was no match for a blue binder filled with paperwork. If he didn't keep the surprise advantage, there was a good chance neither he nor the woman would live to see tomorrow.

Thankfully, she caught on and returned her gaze to the gunman. She pleaded with him. "I'm telling you. I don't know what you are looking for. I don't know what you want. I don't know anything."

"Liar," the gunman said, with such force and venom Cooper feared he only had a few seconds more.

"I promise."

A few steps away, Cooper realized the man was even taller than he appeared from across the lobby. Cooper stood 5'10" and this guy towered him by at least half a foot. Maybe more. He'd hoped to swing the binder at the guy's head, but feared with the man's height, he might not connect hard enough at such a steep angle. He had to stun the guy enough if there was any hope of getting that gun away from him.

"Tell me again what you're looking for," the woman said, clearly stalling to give Cooper time to do something. Anything.

"What the—" the man startled, shifting to turn around.

It was now or never. Cooper swung the binder as hard as he could at the guy's right arm, the arm holding the gun.

The gun fell and skidded away from the trio.

"Run," Cooper yelled in the direction of the woman, though he didn't take his eyes from the man.

The man spun the rest of the way around, his left fist directed toward Cooper's face. It was an awkward lefthanded punch from a righthanded guy, but still Cooper was only able to partially block the man's fist as it barreled toward him.

It connected with Cooper's right cheekbone, sending waves of pain through his entire face to the back of his head. Cooper dropped the binder and stumbled a step back. Then got his footing and went for the man's gut.

He saw it coming and started to twist away. Even so, Cooper's fist landed with a solid thud. It wasn't centered enough to knock the wind out of him but he felt it, Cooper was sure of that.

"Die," the man hissed low and drew his right arm back.

Before the man could execute his punch, Cooper connected a quick jab to the guy's throat. The guy might be too tall for a good face punch, but he was the perfect height for Cooper to land a solid punch to his Adam's apple.

The man staggered, grabbing his throat. Cooper was sure he'd go down. Instead, the man stopped, got his footing, then rushed forward, charging like a linebacker, knocking Cooper off his feet. Just like a linebacker's tackle, they both went down hard. Cooper's head hit the floor, and his vision went black for an instant. He felt the man roll off him, both panting.

"Stop," he heard the woman say. "Stop or I'll pull the trigger."

Cooper looked toward the direction of her voice and saw the woman standing over the two of them. Gun in hand. Even from his position on the ground, he saw the gun quake.

Cooper turned to the man on the floor next to him, his vision still black at the edges. The man ignored or didn't hear her. With one hand clasped at his throat, Cooper watched the man scramble to a standing position. Then he heard feet hitting the floor as he ran toward the front exit.

Cooper pushed himself to a seated position. The room spun, and he closed his eyes. He reached up and felt a knot forming on the back of his head, but not the warm liquid of blood. "I thought I told you to run," he said to the woman.

Tires squealed in the front parking lot. Whoever the tall man was, he was gone. Cooper wondered again what he had stumbled into.

He slowly opened his eyes and was surprised to see the gun still pointed squarely at him. The woman stood only a few feet away. He tried to stand. "Don't move," she said, the gun trembling, her finger on the trigger.

"Okay," Cooper said and remained seated.

"Who are you?" she demanded.

The question—the last five minutes, the day, the last eight weeks, really, the last year—angered him then exploded out. "Me?" he said. "Who am I?" He stood, which put him only a foot away from the end of the gun with the world spinning. He didn't care. "Who am I?" he said again. "Who the hell are you?"

Two

"You are sure you don't know what he wanted?" the female police officer asked. Annabeth still couldn't think straight. Things were a blurry jumble in her mind, and there was so little to tell. She had no idea what any of it was about. When she didn't reply, the officer added, "And you never saw the man before?"

"Never," Annabeth said. She was just thankful to be alive. She also found herself asking why she ever thought moving to Alaska was a good idea, questioning every decision she ever made.

Annabeth subtly shifted to get a better view of the man who'd saved her life. He sat, slumped, in the only corner of Rescued Paws' lobby with seating, pressing an icepack to the back of his head. Every few minutes, he moved it to his cheek. Then back again. The male patrol officer of the male/female team sat across from him taking notes as, she presumed, he told his version of events.

Could she be any stupider? She felt like such an idiot. How did she not recognize her own boss? Sure, she had started as the accountant at Rescued Paws only six weeks earlier, and today was his first day back after an extended personal leave. But that was no excuse. His photo was in the company newsletter, wasn't it? And she'd read a year's worth when she started the job, hadn't she?

"Ma'am?"

"Yes, sorry." Annabeth turned her attention back to the officer.

"I asked if you were absolutely certain—one hundred percent—that you don't know what he wanted," she repeated.

"Yes, ma'am, Officer. I'm absolutely certain. One hundred percent." Annabeth answered that question for the eighth time. First, Malcolm Cooper had asked multiple times as they waited for the police to arrive after calling 911. Then, the police officer had asked multiple times. Why did no one believe her? She'd already gone through the entire story with the officer once, but saw doubt on the woman's stoic face. So, Annabeth started from the beginning. Again.

"I was in my office. I thought I was the only one in the building. This guy comes in with a gun. No idea how he got in, because the doors are supposed to be locked when we close at six p.m. He was looking for something or thought I had something. I don't know. He tells me to get up and pushes me here." Annabeth spread her hands to indicate the lobby. "I assumed he was going to try to kidnap me or something. But then, Mr. Cooper shows up. I didn't even know he was at work today. Anyway, they struggle, and the guy's gun is knocked away. They struggle more until the guy gets up and runs out the same door you guys came in." She pointed to the front door, though her eyes went to where her boss and the other officer sat. "Then we called you." Annabeth took in a deep breath, exhausted by the effort of retelling it. "I swear, I don't have the first clue about what he wanted or who he was. I promise I would tell you if I did."

"Wait here," the officer said.

Annabeth watched as the officer walked to the middle of the large lobby and stopped. She signaled to her partner. Probably wanting to check to see if their stories matched. Annabeth looked at her boss, the icepack now on his cheek. She knew from talk around the office that, even though his first name was Malcolm, everyone called him Cooper. She couldn't help but wonder what the story was behind that fact.

Despite the bloodshot eyes, the swollen red cheek, not to mention how rude and abrupt he'd been with her as they waited following their 911 call, she also couldn't help but notice how good looking he was. On the tall side—though not next to the skinny bad guy—with the wide chest of an athlete, probably near her age or a few years older, a head with short butterscotch waves, and eyes so dark they almost looked black.

What's wrong with you? she chided herself. *You made a fool of yourself once. When will you learn?*

When the police arrived, the first thing they'd done was call paramedics to take a look at Cooper. The paramedics wanted him to go to the hospital for a head scan, but he'd refused. Eventually, they left. The male officer took Cooper to the seating area while the female officer led Annabeth to the opposite corner of the lobby, near the hallway from where Cooper had emerged, the hallway where both his and her offices were. How had she not known he was in his office all day long?

The male officer walked toward his partner. They spoke in a low tone so Annabeth couldn't make out what they were saying. She tried not to be obvious, but she was intently trying to hear their conversation.

Both officers looked her way and she lowered her eyes as if she hadn't been trying to eavesdrop. She looked up again and this time caught Cooper looking back at her. She hadn't even realized her eyes had drifted that way.

The officers motioned her over and they went to where Cooper remained seated. The officer who'd taken her statement said, "Mr. Cooper, are you sure you don't want to go to the hospital? You really should."

"I'm fine," he said dismissively.

"I think we have everything we need for now." The officer retrieved two business cards from her vest pocket and handed one to each of them.

"Can you tell us anything?" Cooper asked.

Without warning, a thought popped into Annabeth's head and she sucked in her breath. The threesome looked toward her.

"Sorry," she said.

"Ms. Neilson?" one of the officers asked.

Annabeth shook her head and looked to the floor.

"Tell us." It was Cooper, his voice softer and kinder than before. Of course, she had pointed a gun at him.

Annabeth raised her eyes and stared into Cooper's. Her stomach fluttered. She shook her head again. It was hunger. It was late. "It's just," she started. "I promise I have no idea who that guy was, but obviously, he knew me. What if...what if he knows where I live?" She meant to sound strong, but she could hear the quiver in her own voice. Why hadn't anyone thought of that earlier?

"Do you have someone you can stay with tonight?" the male officer asked.

She had no one. Not anymore. "No, not here. I'm from Kansas and that's where my parents are. Plus, it's late," Annabeth said, tapping on her wrist as if she wore a watch. "I guess I could get a few things and stay at a hotel tonight."

"But wait," Cooper said before either officer could respond. "She shouldn't go back to her house alone. Even if it's just for a few minutes to get things to take to a hotel."

Great. Annabeth, envisioning worst case scenarios, agreed.

"We'll follow you home," the female officer said. "My partner and I will make sure no one is in your house. Then you can grab a few things and we'll follow you to the hotel."

"Okay," Annabeth said, even though she wasn't feeling very confident. She kept envisioning that gun pointed at her, the guy's gravelly smoker's voice, and his bushy hair. She didn't want to imagine what might have happened if Cooper hadn't been in the building.

The other officer added, "We'll drive your neighborhood. I know neither of you saw the perpetrator's vehicle, but you never know. We'll circle back a few times during the rest of our shift. Just in case."

That helped, a little. "Thank you," Annabeth said. "I'll get my coat and things from my office."

Annabeth watched as Cooper stood, still a bit unsteady. But when the officers asked after him again, he gave the same reply as before. He was fine.

The two walked across the lobby together and then down the hall where Cooper had so fortuitously come from hours earlier. The hallway was T-shaped so, at the end, he went right to his office while she went left to hers.

In her office, Annabeth locked her file cabinets, turned off her computer and adding machine, then collected her bag and put on her coat. In less than five minutes, she started back to the lobby.

There was a flurry of activity when she got there. She couldn't make out the words, but both officers' radios were squawking. Whatever was happening, it sounded important and urgent.

"Is everything okay?" she asked.

"No ma'am," the female officer said as the male officer ran toward the front door. "My partner is getting the cruiser. I'm sorry to say, we have to go. We cannot accompany you to your house. But if you go to the hotel now, we'll call you when we're done. Then we'll accompany you to your house to get your things."

Others needed them, probably people who were way worse off than she. She wasn't listed in the phone book and there was no reason to think the gunman knew where she lived. Or even knew her name. Still, when the officer said that, Annabeth had to clench her teeth to keep from crying. She was just so scared. It was starting to sink in. She'd had a gun pointed at her!

None of what she desperately wanted to say came out. Instead, she just said, "But I don't know what hotel."

"You have my card?"

Annabeth held up the card to indicate she did.

"As soon as you check in, call me and leave a message. Tell me what hotel and what room number. We'll call your room when we're on our way."

"How long will it be?"

"Cannot say, ma'am," the officer said. The cruiser pulled up to the front door, the lights already flashing. "A couple hours maybe."

Because she didn't want to cry, she bit her tongue and watched the officer jog to the front door, push her way through and jump into the passenger side of the cruiser. The sirens blared on and the cruiser sped off.

Three

"Here, take these," Annabeth returned to her living room with a tall glass of water and four Advil tablets. "You must be hurting."

"Thank you," Cooper said, looking up from where he sat on the couch. He shouldn't have done that. Smiling hurt his cheek. Looking up hurt his whole head. It felt like ball bearings cutting a path from the front to the back of his brain. Annabeth was right. His entire head throbbed.

At the office, a 14-hour day had turned into well over a 16-hour one by the time the police sped away. Add in a pounding head, a sore face and no food since breakfast. Cooper felt himself crashing as he'd gone back to his office to gather his belongings. But as soon as he'd turned the corner into the lobby, he saw the officers gone and Annabeth wiping the corners of her eyes. He knew crashing would have to wait.

After she repeated what the cops had said, despite his exhausted mind and battered body, he offered to follow her home, because after all she'd been through, the last thing she needed was to wait several hours for the comfort of her own pajamas. It was just the right thing to do. Not to mention, she was one of his employees, which also made it his responsibility.

When she had gratefully accepted, the corners of her mouth turned up. It wasn't exactly a smile. But it was enough that for the first time since the whole ordeal began, he saw she had dimples. Her face must shine when she genuinely smiled, he thought.

While he finished the glass of water, she retreated to the kitchen and returned with a bag of frozen mangos. "For your head," she said. He looked from the bag to her. "I don't have ice trays. Or frozen peas. Or a slab of steak." Who doesn't have ice? He exchanged the empty glass for the bag of mangos. The mangos amused him, but he didn't say anything, grateful for a cold bag to press to his head. He leaned back into the cushions of the couch.

"It smells delicious," he said, barely able to keep his eyes open.

"It'll be just a few more minutes," she said and, once again, retreated to the kitchen.

Part of the reason he had agreed to stay a little longer when she offered dinner was because he'd lived on fast food and microwave dinners for the better part of two months. But really, the real reason he agreed to stay after he'd looked around her apartment to confirm no one was lurking was the rigidity of her body and the depth of fear in her face. She couldn't hide it. Even her voice quivered when she told him she'd be fine and he could go. She was so clearly not fine and, while going to the hotel would keep her safe, it wouldn't do anything to make her feel less shaken.

At that exact moment when she was telling him she'd be fine, the fact that he hadn't eaten since breakfast made itself known. His stomach made an embarrassingly loud grumble. "I need to eat," he said. "Look, neither of us has had dinner. Why don't we order a pizza or something? That way I can get something in my stomach while sticking around another hour or so just to make sure no one comes by. Maybe by then the police will be done with whatever they have going on."

She didn't reply.

He knew she was scared but didn't know how to read the silence. "Or, why don't I just go?"

"No, it's not that," she said. "I really don't want to go to a hotel and I appreciate your offer to stay a bit longer, it's just—"

"What?"

"Well, it's my fault your whole evening got screwed up," she said as they stood in the center of her living room. She had raised her hand and brought it toward his face, though didn't make contact before she put her hand down again. "It's still so red and swollen. It's going to bruise."

"I grew up with three brothers. I've had worse," he said. How could she say it had been her fault? Unless...he couldn't help but wonder if she were hiding something. Maybe she did know the tall scrawny man or what he was after.

"I wasn't so lucky. I'm an only child. But, how about if I cook something rather than delivery?"

"That's too much hassle after this day."

"It's no hassle. Actually, if you like curry, I made a big pot of curry stew last night. I only need to heat it up. Plus, it's easier because I'm vegetarian. Most people hate sharing a meatless pizza with me." She grinned enough for him to see those dimples again. It was hard to say if he'd been seduced by the dimples or the thought of filling his belly with a homecooked meal. "Plus, you could probably use some Advil and ice for the swelling."

"I love curry," he said. "Thank you."

"No. Thank you."

She'd told him to sit while she put it on the stove.

The truth was his head was pounding more than he wanted to admit. Sitting. Ice. Advil. It all sounded better than a drive across town to an empty house with nothing but canned beans and freezer-burned hotdogs wrapped in equally freezer-burned bread for dinner.

And there was a third reason he agreed to stay—though homemade food and waiting for her to feel less scared were enough. When the paramedics insisted he go to the hospital for a CT scan to rule out a brain bleed and he refused, they made him promise not to be alone and to stay awake for the next few hours. He made the promise with no intention of being able to keep it. At least this way, he could.

Thirty minutes later, he startled awake, and it took a second for his brain to figure out where he was and to remember the events of the past few hours. A covered bread basket sat on the coffee table as well as two cloth napkins and fat soup spoons. Another glass of water sat in front of him. He must've nodded off. So much for staying awake. The pills had taken effect and his head no longer felt like a freight train racing from front to back. Now it was just a small passenger train. Though the pills weren't nearly powerful enough to take away all the pain, or even most of it, he knew a lot more were in his future.

"You're awake," Annabeth said as she entered the room with an orange ceramic bowl in each hand. "Perfect timing." She handed one bowl to him. "Careful, it might be hot. The mangos are back in the freezer, in case you're wondering. They fell on the floor when you dozed off."

"I didn't realize I fell asleep. Thanks," he said, cupping his hands over hers to take the bowl. She took a seat with her own bowl on the other end of the couch.

They hardly spoke as they ate. It was so good, it actually made him sad to remember how long it had been since he'd had a homecooked meal, not counting funeral casseroles his mother's friends and neighbors dropped off. Sad to remember the last eight weeks. The last year. He took his third piece of naan from the bread basket and ran it around the empty bowl to pick up the last of the stew.

"More?" she asked.

He didn't want to make a pig of himself, but another bowl sounded so good.

"It's no problem. I heated up plenty," she said, as if she had picked up on his hesitancy. And before he could politely decline, she was up and taking his bowl back to the kitchen.

Halfway through his second bowl, Cooper finally started to feel satiated. He took in a loud deep breath and leaned back on the couch. "That was amazing. And I'm not just saying it because I was starving."

"Glad you liked it," she said. "It's not hard. I could give you the recipe."

"I can't believe I didn't say two words to you while I ate. My apologies."

She laughed, really laughed. "Apologize? Are you kidding? Let's see. You're going to have a bruised face. I'm sure you have a lump on the back of your head. You came over here when I know you didn't really want to. So, I think the least—the very least—I could do is forgive the lack of dinner conversation."

He'd been right. Her smile lit up her entire face. "So tell me about yourself," he said. Then he remembered he was still her boss and asking was probably illegal in any context. "I mean, tell me how you came to work at Rescued Paws. A lot happened in my absence."

And just like that, the light switched off. You'd have thought he had asked for a kidney.

He watched as she recovered quickly, trying to hide her obvious discomfort. "Not much to tell, really," she answered. "I started at Gibson & Gellar while I was at Alaska Pacific University. Nothing glamorous. I was a part-time office gofer, but it paid better than the jobs on campus. It sparked my interest in accounting, so, since I was a little directionless, that's the degree I got. I planned to return to Kansas when I graduated, but they offered me a job. Even though I'd moved away from home to attend college—APU gave me the best scholarship and financial-aid package—I decided to stay. I do love the Alaska summers. Then a decade after I started, I decided maybe it was time to spread my wings. I saw the ad for Rescued Paws, and here I am."

He stared, trying to read her expression, but it gave nothing away. Cooper believed she wasn't lying, but he got a sneaking suspicion it wasn't the full story either. "A decade? How old are you?" he asked, then immediately knew he had wandered into the illegal territory. He should take it back.

She smiled again. "It's because I'm short," she said, finishing the last spoonful of stew in her bowl. She put it on the coffee table then tucked her feet under herself.

Cooper shook his head, not understanding.

"At least that's my theory. I'm short so people end up thinking I'm a lot younger than I really am. I began working for them during my freshman year."

"So, you're twenty-eight? Twenty-nine?"

"Twenty-eight."

He hadn't thought much about the fact that she was short. Maybe because when he first saw her, she stood with her arms raised above her head. Why had he assumed her to be so much younger? She certainly wasn't immature. Then he realized what it was. "It's the dimples, I think," he said.

"Those too," she said.

He wanted to ask a million more questions. Instead, he leaned forward and took up his bowl. "I think there's still a little more room. It would be bad manners to leave a half-eaten bowl."

"I'm glad for the company. I think I'm finally feeling a little steadier." She held out her hand to test if it shook. It didn't appear to. "I've never been held at gunpoint," she said.

"Do you mind if I ask what you told the police?"

"I don't mind, but the truth is not much. I was in my office. The guy came in with a gun."

"And you never saw him before?"

"How do you think he got in?" she said, ignoring his question. "Zoey was the last to leave at closing. She came in my office to say goodnight and said she'd lock the doors on her way out."

What should he make of her avoidance of his question? Cooper wondered. But said, "Maybe she forgot."

"That has to be it," she said. "None of us realized you were even in the office today."

"Yeah, I had so much work to catch up on, I went in early, closed the door and didn't move until I went into the lobby and saw you."

They were silent for a moment, nothing but the tiny ting sound of his spoon scraping the bottom of the bowl.

"Oh. And, no, I never saw him before," she added, as if just remembering his question.

"What did he want?" Cooper asked.

"This is the strangest part. I don't know. I know it's hard to believe, but I really don't. It seemed like he expected me to know."

"What exactly did he say?" Cooper placed his empty bowl on the coffee table.

"More?" she asked.

"No room." Cooper leaned back and, this time, turned his body to face her on the other end of the couch. "Thank you. It's been a long time since I've had something that good. And filling." He patted his stomach.

"Well, if that's true, it's just sad," she said.

More question avoidance? "You don't have to talk about it if you don't want. I'm just thinking that if we knew what this was about, we could figure out who he was." Then added, "Since you said you don't know him."

She sat quiet for a solid minute. Slowly, she shook her head. "I *do not* know him. I swear. You think I don't know how this sounds? I know it sounds evasive, ridiculous, unbelievable. I know it makes no sense that I absolutely do not know what he wanted."

"I'm sorry," he said. He was sorry. He didn't mean to upset her more than she already was. But he wanted her safe. The only way to do that was to find out who the stranger (if, indeed, he was a stranger) was and what he was after and, most importantly, get him into police custody. And that was true, regardless of whether she was telling him everything or not.

"Maybe the police will be able to trace the gun back to him."

He debated telling her what he already knew to be true. Maybe if he opened up a little to her, she'd do the same. "The gun will probably be a dead end."

"What? Why? I mean, how do you know?" she stammered.

"He wore gloves so it's unlikely there are fingerprints to find. Then, while we were waiting for the police, I looked at it. The serial number had been filed off. Did you notice?"

She shook her head no. After he'd gotten the shaking gun from her hand—after telling her who he was—she'd stood zombie-like far from him, far from the gun as they waited for the police to arrive. Of course, she didn't notice.

"If you believe television, they should be able to spray a magic mystery chemical, put on protective eyewear and a minute or two later—poof—the serial number. A minute more and—poof—the computer spits out the guy's name, where he lives, works, and what he had for breakfast this morning."

The corners of her mouth turned up, but it wasn't genuine. She wasn't in the mood for funny. He had the strongest urge to move across the couch and take her in his arms. Not in a sexual way—though there was no denying she was sexy—but in a protective way. He wanted her to feel everything would be all right. Even if neither of them could say for sure it would be.

"Even if they were able to get the serial number, I'm betting it isn't legally registered," he said. "Maybe a good night's sleep will clear your mind. Maybe you'll remember something tomorrow."

She stood so abruptly he knew he'd gone one step too far. She was angry. "How many times do I have to say it? I told the cops. I told you. I don't know anything." She grabbed for his bowl, stacked it on her own, added the empty bread basket to the tower and, with her free hand, took up his water glass. "Do you want a cup of hot tea?" she asked in a softer voice, forcing the corners of her mouth upward. Despite the effort, it was no smile.

That surprised him. He expected he was about to be asked to leave. Cooper supposed her fear exceeded her revulsion of him at the moment. "Sure."

"Chamomile, okay? I think it'll help me sleep."

"That's fine." Cooper wasn't much of a tea guy, but the offer had little to do with tea. Thoughts swirled around in his mind as he replayed the events at Paws.

He listened as Annabeth prepared the tea. The distinct clicking of a gas stove lighting. The water running, filling a kettle. He leaned back against the cushions, wishing for the bag of mangos, and closed his eyes again. He replayed what she'd said. What little she'd said. He thought about the way her face changed so drastically when he asked her to tell him about herself. What was this short, lovely woman with the bright eyes and dimples hiding?

Four

Preparing the tea gave Annabeth the few minutes she needed to calm down. He was so infuriating. Both he and the police thought she knew the guy. She didn't. And she had no idea how to convince them of that fact. Was there something about her that was inherently untrustworthy?

Annabeth returned to the living room carrying a tray that included two mugs of tea, with the square paper dangling from the tea bags, as well as two spoons, a small pitcher of coconut milk, and several sugar cubes on a saucer.

She wanted to still be irritated, but she couldn't help but smile when she found him asleep again. This sleep was deeper than before. His slow rhythmic breathing told her he was down for the count. Unless she woke him.

She quietly placed the tray on the coffee table and stood looking down at him.

She should wake him and tell him to go home, to assure him she was okay. It was true, she was feeling less shaky, less anxious.

Better still, she should tell him to go home and then drive herself to a nearby hotel just as the police advised. But she didn't have the heart to wake him or the desire to leave the familiarity of her own place. Instead, she went to her bedroom where she retrieved a quilt from where it hung over the back of a chair. The one with blue icebergs and occasional polar bears and burgundy trim in the eight-pointed star pattern quilt her mother had made to keep her warm in Alaska. She also snagged a pillow from her bed.

She set the pillow at the end of the couch where she'd been sitting. Then she opened the quilt and gently laid it over Cooper. She wondered again why people called him Cooper, his last name, instead of Malcolm, his first. Malcolm was a nice name, she thought.

Her insides stirred as she looked down at him. Even with the red swollen cheek, he was quite nice to look at. That wavy hair made her want to reach out to see if it was as soft as it appeared.

His prodding had annoyed her, but as he lay there, not questioning her, she had the strong urge to stroke his face. Kiss the red swollen cheek.

Stop, she chided herself. *Just stop. It's not real.* These were fake feelings tied to the fact that he likely had saved her life hours earlier. It's gratitude. Nothing more.

Still, there was no denying his rugged good looks. From what she'd gathered around the office during her first six weeks, he was a good person. Her co-workers genuinely seemed to enjoy working for him. Of course, she had to remind herself that she was still in the honeymoon phase, that period during a new job where people were polite but distant because you weren't part of the gang yet. It also meant she wasn't in on the office gossip. The reality was he could be a terrible person.

Annabeth looked down at Cooper as he shifted, sinking further into the couch cushions. *Just keep telling yourself that*, she said to herself. *He's probably a terrible person.*

She took her mug of tea and dropped in a sugar cube. She left the tray with everything on it where it was and went into her bedroom. The tea went down fast and the warmth relaxed her. Then exhaustion overcame her. No wonder. It was well after midnight.

Annabeth crawled into bed, telling herself not to replay the horrible scary events of the evening. Erase the image of the gun pointing straight at her. The rough growl of the man who was so sure she had what he wanted. Easier said than done. It was impossible not to keep hearing over and over again, "Tell me." Oh, she would've if she could've.

Despite the exhaustion, sleep proved elusive. No matter what she told herself, she kept seeing the gun, the man, hearing the voice, watching as he and Cooper hit the ground hard. She wondered if she should've shot him when she had the chance. At least this would be over and the fear might begin to dissipate.

What if Cooper hadn't been there? What if he hadn't come into the lobby at that exact moment? She could be dead right now. The idea of how much worse tonight could've been made her shiver even under the two heavy blankets.

~ * ~

Annabeth's ringtone, though set low, caused her eyes to fly open and her body to go rigid. Her heart pounded. Had she been dreaming? She grabbed the phone from her nightstand.

"Ms. Neilson?" a female voice said.

"Umm, yeah, sorry. Hello?" Annabeth whispered into the phone. Her voice raspy from the abruptness of waking up after only—she looked over at the digital clock on her nightstand—after only six hours of sleep. Or, after six hours of lying in bed. Probably only a couple hours of sleep.

"It's Officer Weir."

It took a second for Annabeth's brain to unscramble enough for the events of the night before to flood back into her consciousness and to remember Office Weir. "Yes, Officer. Good morning. Any news?"

"Not yet. I was actually calling as promised. My partner and I wanted to come by the hotel and escort you home. You didn't leave a message so I'm not sure which hotel," she said. "I apologize for how long it took. I'm sure you'll see why on the news later today. We only just finished."

"The escort? Oh, right. It's no problem. Actually, I'm okay. My boss followed me home and then stayed the night."

"Oh?" the officer said.

Annabeth felt herself flush. "No, no. Not like that. He stayed on the couch."

"So you're okay?"

"Yes. I'm not sure what I'll do tonight. That lunatic is still out there."

"My partner and I are heading back to the station now. We'll write up the report and turn it over to the detective squad for followup." Annabeth could hear the officer's radio static in the background and then it abruptly shut off. "Sorry about that," she said. "Later this afternoon you should get a call. They'll probably ask you to go over everything again and they'll want to talk to Mr. Cooper."

Annabeth waited for her to say something reassuring. She hoped to hear a promise of finding the guy, of preventing him from coming after her again. Anything.

"Okay," she finally said. "I'll wait to hear from them, then."

She dropped back onto her pillow. She felt hungover. Like she did after a full night of drinking. Not that she'd done much of that, even as a teenager. Everything hurt. Her eyes. Her head. She ached. She was tired. Her insides felt like acid. She felt—as her grandmother used to say—rode hard and put away wet. Annabeth never understood that expression and, still, somehow, it described exactly how she felt.

The alarm wouldn't go off for another hour, but she knew sleep, no matter how fatigued she felt, would be impossible. Her body was exhausted but her mind was in spin mode.

After showering and slipping on her fluffy, thick Winnie-the-Pooh bathrobe, she opened her bedroom door with the idea of tiptoeing to the kitchen to start coffee. But a glance into the living room told her tiptoeing wasn't necessary.

Cooper was gone.

She stopped and noticed he'd folded the quilt and stacked it on the pillow. The tea tray was gone. It was an odd feeling. She was unsure if she was relieved or disappointed. Or maybe a little scared and angry?

In the kitchen, she found the tray next to the sink and the empty mug in the sink. She turned to the opposite counter to start the coffee, but what she found was a sticky note attached to it.

Good morning. Sorry for falling asleep last night. I hope you were able to get some rest. It's 5:45 and I'm heading home for a shower and then to the office. If you need to take the day off, no worries. I understand. C.

There was a little arrow on the bottom that told her to turn the note over. So, she did.

P.S. Coffee is ready. Just push start.

So she did that, too.

~ * ~

Annabeth arrived at the office before 8, a Rescued Paws insulated mug filled with coffee as well as a container with the last of the curry stew in hand. She was surprised to be the fourth to arrive after Shannon, Zoey and Cooper. She parked next to Cooper's truck, which she recognized from driving him to it the night before. The office didn't open for pet adoptions until 9:00 and most days, most of the staff arrived then, too. Of course, it was December and there were a lot of year-end tasks and deadlines.

She thought about taking Cooper up on the offer to stay home. But with rest proving to be impossible, that would just leave her with a spinning mind. No. Weird as it felt after the events of the night before, work was the best option.

She couldn't say why, but walking in the front door, Annabeth suddenly felt awkward, even embarrassed. Maybe it was because Cooper was a good guy. Maybe it was because no man had ever prepared coffee for her. It was silly, she told herself. Stupid. She couldn't be attracted to her boss. She simply wouldn't allow it.

Hadn't her last big problem started the same way? Minus the gunman and the hand-to-hand combat. Didn't she end up here—at Rescued Paws—being held at gunpoint, because of an inappropriate attraction? *Stupid*, she thought again.

She put the stew in the kitchen's refrigerator and made a beeline across the lobby for the hallway to her office. At the T, she forced herself not to look right toward Cooper's office. She turned left and headed straight for hers. When she emerged an hour later to refill her coffee mug, she actually peeked outside her office before heading down the hall. Why was she avoiding Cooper? He'd been nothing but kind to her. Well, if you discounted the endless probing about whether or not she knew the gunman.

She hoped not to find him in the lobby as she walked through on her way to the little kitchen. What was wrong with her? This feeling was a bit like the infamous walk of shame. But that was dumb; she had nothing to be ashamed of. She was the victim. They were the victims. No matter how it felt, this was not the walk of shame. This was awkwardness. The walk of shame was something she knew all too well. Something she'd done way too many times during her last year at Gibson & Gellar.

She breathed a sigh of relief when she found only the intake desk volunteer in the lobby. But coming out of the kitchen, which stood halfway between the intake desk and the front door, her luck ended. She spotted Cooper leaning over the counter talking to the volunteer. Darn it.

Even though she'd just finished telling herself there was nothing to feel funny about in seeing him again, she turned and walked the opposite way from the pair. She ducked into the overnight drop-off room. Could she be any more of a coward? A dork?

She closed the door softly to ensure no one heard it, then leaned into it, listening. *Now what?* She pressed her forehead to the cool metal door.

Annabeth jumped when she heard a noise behind her. She turned to find a black bundle of energy in the floor-level cage behind her. She had assumed the room was empty.

"Hi, little one," she said, setting the mug on the counter across from the stacked cages. She bent over and opened the cage door.

The black ball of fluff burst out, tripped over her feet, squiggled like a worm and started yipping in delight. Clearly a puppy. She was so excited and happy her tail made her entire back half shake.

"Shh," she said, squatting down to pet the pup.

The tiny room had been added on to the building next to the front entrance for people to drop off dogs they either found or were relinquishing during non-business hours. In the first week at Paws,

Annabeth learned the reason for the room. A terrible story from one winter a decade ago when someone tied three dogs to Paws' front door on a particularly cold night. Too cold for them to survive until morning.

The small, heated room with two kennels for large dogs and stacked cages for small dogs and cats had been built with two doors, the one she'd come through from the inside of the building and one from the parking lot. The door, Annabeth suddenly thought. The door. Could the gunman have gotten into the building through the drop-off room door?

But as quickly as the idea came, she dismissed it. While the door to and from the parking lot would have been unlocked last night at 8:00, the room's second door to the lobby—the one she'd just come through—automatically locked from this side of the door. It remained locked from the inside at all times. A key was needed to get back into the lobby. As a double confirmation, Annabeth looked up at the door's lock, but there was no sign of someone trying to jimmy it.

Another thought came in quick succession. A dreaded thought. She didn't have her own keys. She'd left her office only to refill her coffee. Who knew she'd be sneaking from the kitchen to the drop-off room to avoid coming face-to-face with Cooper? That meant she'd be heading outside into the December cold and still-dark morning in order to get back in through the front door. Without a coat. It was only 9:00 a.m. and she was already having a very bad day. After a very bad night.

The black dog smothered her hand in kisses to get Annabeth's attention, a signal she'd stopped stroking it.

"Little one," she said again. It was against protocol to remove the dog from a cage, but since that ship had already sailed, what would a few minutes of play hurt? Annabeth extended her legs out in front of her to sit on the floor. In an instant, the bouncing black puppy climbed all over her, licking, biting the sleeve of her sweater, in the spastic floppy way only puppies do.

"What's your name and how did you end up here?" Annabeth asked. "How could someone drop off a pup as cute as you?"

After a few minutes, the puppy started to calm and Annabeth got a good look at her sweet face, which was all black with soft brown eyes. All black, that is, except for the small white patch over one eye in the shape of a parallelogram. Parallelogram? Where had she pulled that from? High school geometry, she thought. Weird. Funny how the mind worked.

Annabeth gathered the puppy in her arms and held her close.

A minute later, Annabeth was taken by surprise when her throat tightened and tears began to fall down her face. What was wrong with her? Normally, at work, she'd fight like crazy to not cry. It's so unprofessional. But she couldn't have stopped if she tried. Not today.

I was held at gunpoint. I could've died. Or worse. Oh my God, I was held at gunpoint.

Annabeth didn't know how long she sat on the cold cement floor holding the puppy close before the tears slowed. The puppy licked at her cheeks.

"Thank you, baby," she said.

When the door behind her opened, it nearly startled her out of her skin.

"Oh," she heard above her. She looked up to see Cooper standing in the doorway. Of course.

"I didn't know anyone was in here," he said. Then his face changed from surprised to concerned. He squatted next her. "Are you okay? What's wrong? Did something happen?"

"I'm okay," she said. "I don't know. It just—" She wiped her face and tried to stand. He took her elbow to help her up. It wasn't easy with the 15-pound dog still in her arms. "I know I'm not supposed to take dogs out of the cages," she said. "But it's just a puppy."

"Don't worry. It's okay," he said. "It's a safety thing and this one looks pretty harmless." Cooper reached over and patted the dog's head, his hand immediately covered in sloppy kisses. The pup's tail thumped hard against her arm in happiness. "Actually, I was just talking to the volunteer. She slipped on the ice yesterday, so I told her I'd open the front door and see if there were any animals out here."

Annabeth handed the dog to Cooper. "How old do you think she is?" Annabeth asked.

"Not very." He lifted her lip to look at her teeth. "Three months, probably," he said. "What name should we give her?"

Annabeth stroked the black fur. "Hmm," she said. She hadn't yet gotten the opportunity to name any of the animals who came to the rescue. "How about Solstice?"

"Solstice? Now, that's a good Alaska name, especially with winter solstice only a couple weeks away."

The minute of conversation gave her enough time to pull herself together. "I should get back to work."

"So what happened?" he asked again. "Are the tears about last night?"

"Nothing. Yeah, probably. I'm fine."

He tilted his head questioningly. He looked genuinely concerned, but she also felt like he was, once again, on the verge of asking if she knew the gunman. Her mind was a swirling mess. "I forgot my keys," she said, picking up her coffee mug and stroking the puppy in his arms one last time.

"Sure," he said, and shifted the dog into his left arm so he could retrieve his keys from his jeans' pocket.

When she got back to the safety of her office and the comfort of her chair, Annabeth took several deep breaths. She shook her head, a little disgusted with herself. She felt equal parts mortified and emotional basket case. She couldn't believe Cooper had caught her crying. Didn't she ever learn? Her work rules were rules for a reason. No crying. No dating co-workers. There were others, but those two were firmly, unflinchingly, at the top of her list. Still, she had to admit, the crying had been a welcome release.

Work, she decided, was the best medicine. The concentration her job required would help her keep out of her own head, away from thoughts of the tall man and the boss man.

At lunch, an early one today because she'd skipped breakfast, she stopped working and headed back to the kitchen to heat her stew in an old microwave oven that took twice as long as it should to heat anything. Back at her desk again, she opened her email program. While she ate, she caught up on correspondence. She saw Cooper had sent a note to the staff about the night before. He downplayed the severity of the incident, but wanted them to be aware and to keep an eye out for anything out of the ordinary. He had to explain about the fight—scuffle was the word he used—because of his red and soon-to-be bruised cheek. He asked anyone who had an idea of what the gunman (though he called him the bad guy and left out the part about the gun) might have been looking for to please talk to him. Also, if anyone felt upset or had questions, they could also talk to him.

Annabeth wasn't sure if she should hope that someone on the staff knew something. She certainly wouldn't wish that anyone else would come in contact with the gunman. But it was good Cooper had shared the information. Just in case.

In the early afternoon, when her eyes burned and watered from the strain of looking at numbers on the screen, Annabeth finally took a real break.

She stood and stretched out the kinks in her back and neck. She massaged her hands and fingers and rolled her wrists. First one way and then the other. Sore wrists were an occupational hazard. Sitting in the same position for the last five hours didn't help either. She walked to her window and looked out at the snow-covered pine trees that spread out thick in the area on her side of the building. It wouldn't be long before it got dark again. She loved Alaska, but winters proved a challenge. She didn't like both arriving and leaving work in the dark four months of the year.

She returned to her chair, leaned back and closed her eyes. She had a random thought about her favorite oversized hoodie. She smiled when the face of the black puppy came to her mind. Then, a minute later, it hit her. Her eyes popped opened, she shot up, her heart thudding in her chest.

Five

"Wait. Wait. I can't understand you," Cooper said after Annabeth burst into his office, a fast flood of words pouring from her mouth.

She paused. Then started again. Unfortunately, it sounded exactly the same. "Whoa, Nelly. Wait. Stop. Take a breath." He watched as she did as he directed. "And another." He stared. Their eyes glued on one another. "Okay, try again. This time slow. With pauses."

She took another deep breath. "I was in my office and bam! I remembered something," she said and took another deep breath.

"What?" he said excitedly.

"I don't know. I mean—" and the rapid-fire words started for a third time, though this time he heard the word *gun*.

Cooper stood and walked around his desk. He took her by the arm and led her to the small round meeting table in one corner of his office. He pulled out a chair for her to sit. Then pulled out the one next to her and sat. "We've got all the time in world," he said, the mound of paperwork on his desk forgotten. "Take your time. I want to understand you."

"Okay," she said. She clasped her hands together and set them on the table, trying to corral the energy that had sent her flying through his office door to begin with. "Sorry."

"Now, what about the gun?"

"All I saw was the barrel pointing straight at me. You know? My whole body felt hollow and that barrel seemed like this giant black hole. It was so big. I couldn't think straight. Cooper, I swear to you, I don't know who that guy was. The first time I saw him was when he came into my office with that gun pointed at me."

"I believe you," he said. He had wanted to believe her last night. And now, maybe he did. She seemed unguarded for the first time.

"It's so strange. I don't know how to describe it. I mean, I don't know if this will make sense."

"Try," he encouraged.

"I was so stunned, then terrified when I realized what was happening. I couldn't think straight," she said again. "My ears were pounding. I remember that. I think the reason I couldn't hardly remember anything is because I didn't hear him. I don't know why I couldn't verbalize that last night. I barely heard anything he said to me. I could see his lips moving but my mind couldn't do anything but focus on that giant gun staring me down."

Cooper wasn't sure how to ask the next question without sounding accusatory because, if last night had been any indication, the wrong question would shut her down completely, close her tighter than a rusty padlock. *Ease into the question*, he told himself.

Cooper reached across the table and put his hand on her arm. "I'm so glad you're okay," he started.

She rapidly blinked away the swell of emotions. Cooper hadn't realized until that moment just how deeply she'd internalized the terror of the night before. Women were different than men. And who was he to say? He wasn't the one looking down the barrel of a gun. But that's what he saw on her face. Terror.

"You're safe," he reassured her.

She swiped at her cheeks as if tears had fallen, though she'd managed to keep them contained.

"When you came in, you said you remembered something. What was it?" He made the effort to keep his voice soft and low. *Gentle*, he told himself.

She bit her lip.

"Maybe it would help if I told you something?"

She met his eyes. "Maybe." Even brimming with tears and starting to redden, she had the brightest blue eyes he had ever seen.

"Last night you told me what happened from your point of view," he said. "But I never told you what happened from mine. Maybe if I tell you how it looked from the outside that will help."

She waited.

"When I got to the lobby, I heard him say—and he said it a bunch of times—'*tell me.*' That's why I got the impression you two knew each other. It was like a shorthand or something, like he thought you were holding back. And I took that to mean—and I can see I was wrong—that you understood what he was after. You kept saying you didn't know what he was talking about, but I thought that was your way of buying time, of not giving him what he wanted. That's how it looked from the outside."

"I think I was in a kind of trance," she said.

"Not a trance. You were in shock, more like."

"Yeah. I just couldn't get my mind wrapped around what was happening, especially since I really didn't understand what he was after. Still don't."

"But you remembered something?" Cooper asked again.

"It's not much. I was so excited to remember anything, I might have built this up way more than it deserves. But now, I kind of remember him saying something about money. And it's weird because I also know he wasn't after *my* money. I mean, my purse was in plain view and he didn't take it. I just wish—ugh, it's so frustrating. Why can't I remember more?"

Cooper wanted her to stay focused. He feared if she spiraled back down again, those nuggets she remembered would be lost. "I'm inclined to agree with you. If it was about robbery, you think he'd go to a bank, a convenience store, someplace he'd know for sure had money."

"I know," she agreed. "The other word I think he said—this one is less clear because it makes even less sense. If that's possible. He said something about—oh, I don't know—about something being certified. Or close to that."

Cooper thought for a moment. He drew a blank. She must've misheard. Rescued Paws was a nonprofit dog and cat rescue, nothing here was certified. Then again, they didn't keep money on hand, and she remembered the man saying the word money. "I didn't think about it until just now, but do you think the guy was on drugs or mentally ill? Maybe that's why none of this make sense."

"I wish I could say I thought that was true, but I didn't get that. Did you?"

"No," he admitted. "He was too focused and clear. I haven't been around addicts much, so I'm not sure I'd know one if I were eating a meal with him. But, even so, I didn't pick up on that either."

They both sat staring at the grain of the wooden table top. When nothing made sense, where do you go next?

"I know it's not much, but you should still tell the police. I'm sure they'd want to know. Speaking of the police, have you heard from anyone today?" Cooper asked.

"Not yet," Annabeth said. "Well, that's not true. I heard from Officer Weir early this morning when they finished with that emergency. She said the case would be turned over to the detective unit. They are supposed to call at some point today."

It was past mid-day already. Cooper thought about this. He once had a neighbor who'd been a police officer before he and his wife moved to southern California for him to attend law school. Cooper remembered at one particular summer barbeque just before they moved, after several rounds of beers, where the guy expressed his frustration with the job.

What had he said?

Unless it was big, the police often could do little more than open a case file.

Surely being held at gunpoint was big. Wasn't it? The more he thought about it, the more he feared the night before would get little police attention. What had really happened? There was no break-in. Or no obvious break-in, anyway. The gun never discharged. Yes,

Cooper had been assaulted. Maybe if he'd gone to the hospital like the paramedics suggested, the case would've risen to a higher level of seriousness. He wished he'd thought of that last night.

It wasn't robbery, since the guy left with nothing. He supposed it was attempted robbery. Maybe something more since a gun was involved. Aggravated robbery? Robbery with a deadly weapon? Who knew? Like most people, everything he knew about criminals was from television. The guy didn't seem to want to take anything. Not Annabeth's purse, anyway. Maybe he was after information. *Tell me* were the words he had repeated. *Tell me*. But, then again, Annabeth remembers him using the word *money*. Cooper shook his head to stop the mind circles.

But, if he were correct, and this amounted to little more than a scuffle from the police's point of view, she'd be lucky to get a cursory follow-up call. The more he thought about it, real action seemed unlikely.

That meant only one thing.

He and Annabeth needed to figure it out. Obviously, the gunman didn't get what he had come for which, Cooper had to assume, meant it wasn't over. That meant Annabeth was at risk. Grave risk. What if he hadn't stumbled on the scene last night? What had the tall man intended to do with her? After all, he led her from her office. Where was he taking her?

His progression of thoughts led to the fact that the man most certainly would be back. "We have to figure this out," Cooper finally said aloud, his voice no longer soft and low but rather, sharp and urgent. Determined.

He startled Annabeth, who'd been lost in her own thoughts.

"Sorry," he said and squeezed her arm where his hand had remained during their entire conversation.

"How? How do we figure this out when none of the pieces makes sense? We know nothing. I know nothing."

Cooper had no idea, so said the only thing that came to mind. "Okay, let's go through it all again from the beginning."

Thirty minutes later, they were no further along. They'd each repeated their version of what happened in as much detail as possible. Cooper's frustration level rose equally with his fear for Annabeth's safety.

"We need to think outside the box," Annabeth offered. "If nothing makes sense, we need to look at it from a different angle."

"Ideas?"

"Well, no, I'm rambling. I'm tired."

"You aren't wrong. What do we know for sure?" Cooper asked.

"One more time. Okay, we are pretty sure it wasn't about him trying to rob me."

"Agreed."

"Ergo, it's not about me."

Cooper couldn't help but laugh. "Ergo?"

She laughed too. "Too much television in my formative years. Sorry. So it may or may not be true, but let's say it is."

"Okay, it's not about you," Cooper repeated back to her.

"If it isn't about me, it begs the question—"

"Who's it about?" Cooper offered.

"No. Well, yes. But, no, that's not what I was thinking. Bear with me. He came into this building at a time it normally would've been locked. It should've been locked."

"True, but the door being locked or unlocked might be irrelevant because surely, if he'd been determined to get in and it was locked, he would've broken in."

"True. But, regardless, it was at a time when no one should've been here. We'd been closed two hours by then. I know it's not neat and tidy, since my car was in the employee parking lot. But on most any other day, neither you nor I would've been in the building at eight p.m. on a Tuesday night. The building would've been empty."

"Anyone could've seen your car. Now I wish I'd parked there. But anyone could've only seen your car if they'd gone around to the back of the building to the employee parking area. And we both saw him leave out the front door. So—or should I say, ergo?—if he assumed no one was in the building, he'd have no reason to go around back to look."

"Exactly," Annabeth said. "Which then circles back again to this: it wasn't about me. I think he was here to find something—still no idea what—and when he found me instead, he just figured I knew where it was or I could find it faster. I mean, if I weren't a new employee, maybe I would've."

"And you have no memory of what, if anything, he said he was looking for?"

Cooper watched as she closed her eyes, sifting through the memory, slowly shaking her head. She opened her eyes, her head still going side to side. "I don't. I wish I did. I feel like he must've said it but I have nothing."

Cooper turned away from her and stared at a spot on the floor to focus his concentration. He went through her idea, looking for holes. It wasn't entirely out of left field. Even so, it didn't get them any closer to knowing who he was or what he wanted. But it was a theory of something and that was more than they had before she suggested they think outside the box.

He met her eyes again. "And yet," he said. "Yet, he came to your office."

"Oh, come on." She pulled her arm out from under his hand. "Don't tell me we're back here again. You said you believed me. I don't know him. I don't know why he came to my office. Maybe he saw the light on. Your door was closed. Mine wasn't. Maybe he heard me. We don't know."

Cooper forgot for a moment. *Gentle.* Or she'd go on the defensive. He reached out and took her arm again. "No, no. I'm sorry. My fault. I didn't mean it how it sounded."

"What did you mean, then?" she demanded, though made no move to pull her arm away, which Cooper took as a good sign.

"Now it's your turn to bear with me. You said he said something about money. He used the word money. What I said badly," he said, then tried again. "What I meant to say was there is a connection between you and money. But it's not about you, the person."

"I don't understand," she said.

"Maybe it's about you, the accountant."

Her face scrunched. "No. You're suggesting it's about Paws' money? I think you're grasping at straws. We're a nonprofit, we have no money."

"Of course I'm grasping at straws," Cooper said. "We have nothing else to grasp at. This was your idea. I'm thinking outside the box." If he didn't want to keep his hand resting on her arm, he might have added air quotes to "thinking outside the box."

Her scrunched face turned into a stifled smile. "I did say that."

"Think about it, he didn't come to my office and I was here, too. Why? My door was closed, granted, but if he were really looking for something that could be anywhere, surely the director's office would be the place you'd start. But he went to your office. The office of the accountant. Also, as you said, he wouldn't have known you are new. That could've been why he thought you knew more."

"But we don't keep money here on hand and I thought our other theory was this wasn't about robbery. Are you saying, if it's not about robbing Rescued Paws, it was simply a terrible, terrible idea on his part?"

Cooper didn't think that was it, but for one moment he liked the idea. If it were a stupid idea from a stupid man, there was a good chance he'd realize it and not return. Cooper wanted to believe Annabeth was no longer in danger. He couldn't say why, but everything in his gut said she still was. Or, he should say, his accountant was still in danger. Of course, it was she, the person, he was concerned about.

Cooper was so frustrated he felt heat rise in his body. It seemed like they were getting somewhere and, yet, they were absolutely nowhere. They only followed the trail right back to where they had started. Had they merely gone in a circle?

Then Annabeth said, "When you have a gun pulled on you and the word money is said..." She was speaking very slowly, as if she were putting together the idea at the same time the words were coming out of her mouth.

"Yes?" he encouraged.

"You can't help but think cash. Money. Cash. Right?" She paused. "Oh, no—" she paused again. "I am so far outside the box on this one I can no longer even see the box."

"Say it anyway," he said.

"There is another kind of money. Sort of."

"I don't understand," Cooper said.

"The other kind of money here in this building is paper money. Money on paper."

"I still don't understand."

"Do you think it could somehow be about the finances of Rescued Paws? That's money, but not cash."

Six

The silly expression *a needle in a haystack* kept popping into Annabeth's mind. It wasn't exactly right but still, with each page she reviewed, she would think it again.

It had seemed like a sound plan when she had left Cooper's office a couple hours earlier. At least it was something. Having a plan gave her a concrete task. It made her feel less of a victim, less like her world was spinning out of control. It dimmed the image of the barrel of the gun ever so slightly.

Actually, it *was* a sound plan. Of course, it assumed the "outside the box" theory they'd spun was somewhere in the vicinity of true. And that was one whopper of an assumption. Because they couldn't come up with anything better, they agreed she'd go back to her office and look at the company financials with an eye for something suspicious, which was a pretty broad non-specific swath.

When anyone is thinking of financial crimes, embezzlement is the first thing that comes to mind. Embezzlement at a nonprofit organization as small as Rescued Paws with the systems they had in place could only be accomplished by the accounting person. Or, at least, the accountant would have to be involved. It was hard to believe that sweet woman, Maggie, whom Annabeth had replaced could embezzle. Maggie had spent two weeks training Annabeth and she had been with the rescue since it started twenty-two years earlier.

Annabeth remembered a training she'd taken years earlier. It wasn't exactly forensic accounting; rather, best practices for small companies. One practice they advised, and that she was considering now, was that the accounting person must take time off. A red flag is an accountant who doesn't take vacations. The idea being they don't want someone else looking at the books they've been cooking.

Annabeth minimized the page she was on and opened payroll. It only took ten minutes to see that Maggie had enjoyed regular vacations, and even a couple of lengthy ones. It was a longshot, anyway.

She closed payroll and maximized the page where she left off. Her computer screen filled with columns of numbers. She rested her chin in her hand and started at the top.

In two hours, Annabeth found no red flags. But two hours was nothing when looking for evidence of a misdeed, unless the criminal is a complete dope who makes no attempt at covering it up.

At Gibson & Gellar, she'd done primarily tax work for clients, except for six months she'd spent in the auditing department when, strangely enough, all four women in the department of seven, got pregnant and took maternity leave at the same time. The experience gave her a few ideas of what to look for.

Still, six months in auditing and forensic accounting were apples and oranges. Adding machines and calculators.

Annabeth looked at the clock. Twenty minutes until 4:00 when she was due to return to Cooper's office. She hated going back with nothing because she didn't want to disappoint him.

But she knew another 20 minutes wasn't going to make a difference, so Annabeth made her way to the lobby. The day's afternoon volunteer sat at the intake desk.

"I'm just getting a puppy fix," Annabeth told her, a woman in her 80s if she were a day, with snowy white hair and a bright green stripe down one side. The woman called it her Bella streak because her great-granddaughter's name was Bella and they'd recently got matching stripes.

"I understand. I got my fix when I arrived," the woman said. Annabeth continued on by without stopping.

Rescued Paws employed only eight paid staff members and couldn't survive without the help of volunteers who donated thousands upon thousands of hours of their time every year. Most fostered animals, but some helped at the office as kennel cleaners, groomers, adoption specialists and covering the intake desk.

Across the lobby from the door she'd escaped into that morning was another door which led to the warehouse. The warehouse took up half the building's space and everything rescue related was there, from pet food to grooming supplies. But the best part was found along the back wall: the kennels and cages for the dogs and cats waiting for foster placement or veterinary care. Animals cycled in and out of the warehouse on a regular basis. Capacity was about a dozen dogs and two dozen cats.

At the moment, things were pretty quiet. With Christmas only a couple weeks away, the rescue would see an increase in adoptions.

In the third kennel, though, Annabeth found who she was looking for. It put a smile on her face.

"Hello," she said softly.

The sleeping black Labrador puppy popped up from her nap and started squealing and bouncing with excitement. The pup stuck her little nose though the chain links. Annabeth pushed two fingers through the hole and tried to pet the dog's snout. Instead, her fingers were swallowed by puppy mouth.

"Ouch," Annabeth cried in faux pain and pulled her fingers back.

She opened the kennel door and the ball of energy tripped over her own feet as she charged Annabeth's legs and fell to the cement floor to expose her pink belly. Annabeth laughed. "You're all elbows and knees, aren't you?" she said and sunk down to the cool cement floor. "I only have twenty minutes."

The puppy, like earlier, was a wild child of movement and excitement. Bouncing on Annabeth, nipping, tail wagging furiously side to side, tongue flailing looking to make contact with any part of Annabeth. This was exactly what she needed. Annabeth soaked it up like a dry sponge forgotten in the corner underneath the kitchen sink. It's no wonder they say people with pets have lower stress levels.

In her six weeks of employment, she'd petted a lot of dogs and a few cats. She only vaguely thought about getting one. For one thing, her apartment didn't allow them. But more than that, she didn't know if she could commit. Pet ownership was a big responsibility. Not that she wasn't responsible. But having another being count on her for everything from food to love, from vet care to exercise? It was a lot. There were posters all over the lobby saying as much.

But there was something about this one. She couldn't say what it was, but at this exact moment, she felt happy. She certainly felt loved and it didn't matter that this dog would be excitedly jumping around, no matter who was sitting on the ground.

Such a cute face. And that white patch on an otherwise black dog, a puppy birthmark. Adorable. Annabeth's mother used to say a birthmark was where an angel kissed a baby before sending her to earth. How many times had she heard that? Every time she wore shorts as a kid and complained about the pink birthmark on her thigh, her mother would remind her that not everyone was lucky enough to be kissed by an angel.

A dog, she suddenly thought, could alert her to an intruder. A dog might help her to feel safe. *No, no.* What was she thinking? *Stop being reactionary.* Then again, it couldn't hurt to ask about the puppy, right?

Annabeth got up and returned the puppy to her bed in the kennel, promising to visit again later.

When she closed the kennel door, she saw something she hadn't noticed earlier. The paperwork on a clipboard attached to the chain-link of the kennel door. The name Solstice neatly printed across the top. She smiled seeing the name.

Back at the intake desk, she asked the Bella streak volunteer what, if any, information she had on Solstice.

The woman informed her that she had been dropped off in the overnight kennel which, of course, Annabeth already knew. She said

Ruthie, the morning volunteer, had called several fosters but hadn't found a place for her yet, but they still had time as the dog needed the all clear from the veterinarian before she could actually be placed. Finding a foster or adoptive home was one of the hardest aspects of the rescue. When they couldn't find placement, animals had to be moved to the city's animal control. Annabeth didn't like to think about that. She especially didn't want to think about that possibility for Solstice.

Annabeth thanked the volunteer and returned to her office for her notes.

Back at the round wooden-top table in Cooper's office, they both sat where they had earlier.

Annabeth wished he would sit across from her instead of next to her. Now that she was calmer, after puppy time, she was more aware of his nearness than she had been earlier in the day. It unsettled her. *Focus*, she scolded herself. And, not for the first time, she reminded herself of the difficult lessons she'd learned from the disastrous way things had ended at Gibson & Gellar.

"Annabeth?" she heard Cooper say. "You okay?"

"Fine. Sorry. Distracted."

"You're safe now," he said, misinterpreting her. His voice was low and soft. That male voice. Strong but gentle. Why did her new boss have to be so nice to look at, so nice to talk to? So nice.

"So, bad news," she said, ignoring him. "I found nothing. But, to be fair, two hours is not nearly enough time to find something, especially when I'm not even sure what I'm looking for. I went five years back and saw no significant spikes or dips in annual income or expenses. I looked at vendors."

A puzzled look played over his brow.

"I looked at vendors because a way to steal money is to create fake invoices. You pay those and, really, you're paying yourself or whoever sent the invoice."

"I see."

"It's an area of possible further inquiry, because there wasn't time to research companies. Even—I just thought of this—if something has been going on a long while, we should research all the companies we do business with to make sure they are legit. Initially I thought five years was far enough back, but maybe it isn't. If something has been going on a long time, it would make sense that I'm not seeing unexplained anomalies in the financials in the last few years."

"Unexplained?" Cooper asked.

"Yeah, you know, like last year when the roof leaked. There were nearly twenty thousand dollars of unplanned, unbudgeted expenses. So, if you look at the financials, you see a blip in spending last year but the blip has an explanation. The roof did leak, right? Got repaired?"

"Got it. Yes, bad leaks. We had to go buy more buckets to catch the water coming in until the roofing guys could start the job," he said. "You really are good at this."

Annabeth looked at him. "Don't sound surprised. Sheesh, I don't know if that's a compliment or an insult—"

"Compliment," he said, before she even finished her sentence. "Of course, it's a compliment. I guess I'm just used to working with Maggie. Working with you is very different."

"Nice save," she teased.

"No, it's the truth. I promise."

"How are we different?" Annabeth wondered.

He waved away the question. "Move on. Let's not get sidetracked. It's not important or relevant."

"Okay," Annabeth said. "Unless," she paused. "Are you thinking she might've been cooking the books? I mean, if something were happening with money. She was here a long time."

"Nothing like that. It never even occurred to me she might be involved. Why? Do you think she could be?"

"At this point, I can't point to anything one way or another, but I'm inclined to think not. But I only knew her those two weeks when she trained me and you never know about another person, do you?"

"I don't know about that," he said "If you're paying attention, I kind of think you do. In my wildest imagination, I just cannot see Maggie being party to anything underhanded. She'd never do anything that would take money away from the animals. Helping animals is why she stayed so long."

"So, like I said, the bad news is no red flags," Annabeth repeated.

"Which means the worst news is we are no further along than when we started down this rabbit hole."

"Exactly. If we are even in the right rabbit hole to begin with."

Cooper yawned and covered it with a laugh. "I don't know about you, but I'm beat."

"I am too," she said, even though she wasn't. She'd been sluggish this morning, but after the coffee had kicked in, she felt fine. That reminded her. "I never said thank you," she said, "for the coffee this morning. At my house. It was perfect. And kind."

"It was nothing," he dismissed.

It was definitely not nothing. At least not to her.

"Oh, hey, have you heard from anyone at the police department in the last few hours?" Cooper asked.

"Not yet. Maybe tomorrow."

Cooper's desk phone rang. "Sorry, I have to take this. I'm waiting to hear back from the board president," he said and went to his desk.

Annabeth yawned. Maybe she was a little tired. She started to stand.

"No. Stay." He motioned for her to sit. "It'll just be a minute."

She lowered herself back into the chair. The idea of sleep made her think of going home. She'd gone all day without thinking what would happen tonight. And even though they had agreed it wasn't about her, the person, she suddenly felt quivery.

Panicky, really, at the idea of going home.

What if last night had, in fact, been about her, the person? What if the gunman knew where she lived? The fact was, despite all their sleuthing, they knew nothing. For all she knew, he could be there waiting right now, waiting for her to get home from work.

"Okay, I'll watch for that email. See you Friday," Annabeth heard Cooper say and watched as he returned the phone to its cradle.

She shot up from her chair so quickly she nearly tipped it over. "I better go. Let you get home and catch up on sleep."

"Whoa, wait a minute. What's going on?"

"Nothing. I mean, you're tired and I've inconvenienced you enough," Annabeth said and started toward the door.

"Stop," he said with such force it caused her to stop in her tracks. She turned to face him. "Look, yes, I'm tired but the phone rang before I could finish what I was going to suggest."

Before he could say anymore, Annabeth blurted out, "I need to go. I'm driving to Whittier to see Maggie."

Seven

Despite her repeated attempts to assure him that she'd be fine, there was no way he was about to let her drive an hour to Whittier alone. Cooper looked across the seat of his pickup at Annabeth as she stared out the window into the gray dark night. He wondered what was going through her mind. He tried to ask when they first got on the road, but she'd brushed him off with, "Nothing." She'd stared out the passenger window, making it impossible for him to see her face.

It had been more than a week since the last snowfall so the roads were clear. Unlike recent years, with temperatures fluctuating between the teens and low 40s after the first snowfall on Halloween, this year it had stayed in the 20s. That's the way he preferred it. Once it snowed, it was best to stay below freezing, otherwise the constant change above and below freezing created ice-skating rinks. In parking lots. In people's own yards. On sidewalks. On the roads. It was a mess and the cause of a lot of accidents and falls. Like their volunteer, Ruthie.

But, even clear, on the curvy road of the Turnagain Arm, it was important he remained alert. An unexpected patch of ice could have disastrous results.

He didn't understand her unflinching need to talk to Maggie. She said if they each agreed Maggie wasn't a source of any funny business—

even if she was—talking to her was a good idea because of her long time at Paws. Maybe she could offer some insight into the financials. Cooper first tried to convince her that the conversation could happen over the phone. That wasn't good enough, she'd said. She wanted to talk to her face-to-face, read her body language. Next, he had tried to talk her into waiting until the next day so she could go in the light of day. But she wouldn't hear of that either, since tomorrow was a work day.

She was steadfast in her determination to go tonight. And he simply couldn't let her go it alone. He was equally adamant in this. He told her he was driving because his pickup had 4-wheel drive, which her sedan did not. He'd told himself he'd keep her safe and that's what he was going to do. Even if it meant driving to Whittier in the dark.

He wished she'd say something. Cooper still wasn't sure what had happened in his office, why she shut down. It was strange. Despite the topic, he rather enjoyed talking to her. He liked their banter, working through "what if" scenarios, trying to put the puzzle together. It had been a long time since he'd felt anything resembling joy, even if only the length of a conversation.

Then it hit him.

She was scared. Her reaction was fear. Again. Seriously, how could he be so dense? So insensitive? She mostly came across as strong and handling the situation, so he kept forgetting how terrifying it must've been for her to be held at gunpoint like that, especially in the minutes before Cooper entered the picture, when she had no idea how it was going to end.

"Do you think Maggie will know anything?" he asked, trying to get her to talk to him.

She turned and looked over at him. Then to the road ahead of them. "I hope so," she said.

At least she didn't return to looking out the passenger window, leaving him only with the back of her head. He'd take what he could get.

"You know," he started. "I never finished what I started to say in my office before the phone rang. I wanted to tell you that I have a perfectly good extra bedroom—two in fact—at my house. You're welcome to stay with me until this thing gets figured out."

She looked to him again but didn't reply.

"I think maybe that's why you wanted to visit Maggie. I mean, is this really a good idea or were you just trying to avoid going home?"

"It is a good idea," she answered. Then added, "Why can't it be both? Or neither. I don't know. Does it matter?"

"I promise, I will keep you safe," Cooper said. "That's really what I wanted to say."

She continued to face forward, her eyes staring straight ahead.

After several more miles, Annabeth said, "Okay, I admit it. This probably is a grand waste of time. But I called Maggie after I left your office and she said it was okay for me to come see her. So, I'm going with the idea that you just never know. I'm standing outside the box here."

"Okay, agreed. But I'm not kidding. It's no problem for you to stay with me when we get back to town if you don't have another place to go, until we're sure that guy won't be coming back. I'll give you a key to come and go as you please."

"I appreciate it," she said, without committing one way or the other.

He hoped she'd take him up on the offer. But he couldn't force her. Boss or no. On the other hand, if she agreed to stay with him, he knew it would take all his willpower not to try to get close to her. Even sitting here in his truck, he fought the urge to take her hand in reassurance.

What was wrong with him? So inappropriate to be thinking about intimacy at a time like this. She was scared. His employee. And so beautiful. And smart. Cooper shook his head to stop the thoughts. But he'd buried his own needs for so long. He tried to convince himself that's what these crazy thoughts were really about.

He was glad to see the turnoff sign. Cooper slowed on the highway and eased left into the Portage Glacier turn lane. Once off the highway and on the narrow two-lane road to Portage and Whittier, he followed the road past closed campgrounds. The tunnel into Whitter was a couple miles past Portage Glacier and its visitors' center, which was a big summer tourist draw. But this time of year, the area was dead quiet.

At the tunnel, he eased up to the fee hut. An Alaska Native woman wearing a thick coat with the fur-rimmed hood up opened the hut window and waited for Cooper to hand over $13. She handed him an information sheet and receipt before telling him to pull into lane number one of the staging area. He stuffed the papers into the nearest cup holder. After the hut, the road spread out into six lanes, based on vehicle size, then merged back into one just before the entrance of the one-way mountain tunnel.

"I've never been here in the winter," Annabeth said. "Actually, I've only been here twice since moving to Alaska."

Cooper pulled into lane one. He put the pickup in park because it was much too cold to turn off the engine. The only other vehicle waiting was a semi-truck in lane six. "What? Only twice? I usually come once or twice a summer. For fishing. Do you like to fish?" Cooper said. He pointed to the clock on his dash and added, "Ten minutes before it opens."

Going into Whittier, the single-lane tunnel opened on the half hour. Leaving the quirky tiny town, the tunnel opened on the hour. Back and forth, day and night. It always reminded Cooper of a very slow game of ping pong. In the winter months, when temperatures were particularly cold, like today, the window for the tunnel opening reduced to five minutes from the normal 15, so he was glad they'd timed it right. If they had missed the window, they'd have quite a long wait.

"I fished a few times as a kid but never here in Alaska, if you can believe that. Now that I'm vegetarian I have no reason to," she answered. "How's your face and head? Hurt?"

"I've kept up on the Advil all day, so not too bad." It wasn't exactly true, but he wasn't about to tell her about the constant throb of his face and the pressure he felt from the swollen baseball-sized lump on the back of his head.

"That's good," she said.

"Yeah," he said. It was followed by a minute of awkward silence. He had finally got her talking and now he couldn't think of anything to say.

"So, do you have any pets?" she asked. "I assume you do, working at a rescue organization and all."

"I had a dog, but I lost him about a year ago and haven't been ready for another one." It wasn't the whole story but every word was true. "You?"

"You've been to my apartment. You know the answer to that."

"Oh, right. Not thinking." He pointed to his head.

"Actually, ever since I started at Paws, I've been considering it. My apartment doesn't allow them, but my lease is up at the end of the month. I've been avoiding signing a new one, thinking maybe I could find a little house with a yard. I don't know. It's probably too late. I'll probably just sign for another six months."

"Dog or cat?"

"What?"

"Which would you get? Or both?"

"Everyone says a cat is a lot less work, but I'm kind of in love with all the dogs I've met in the last few weeks. Like that one today."

"Solstice? Labs make great pets. I had two growing up," Cooper said. "Bruce and Wayne." He then went on to tell her about his superhero dogs.

A honk came from behind them. An SUV had pulled into lane one and he hadn't even noticed. The traffic light hanging from the wire overhead had turned green. Cooper put the truck into gear and headed to the tunnel's entrance to travel the two-and-a-half miles through the mountain into Whittier.

"It's so eerie in here," Annabeth said once inside the tunnel.

It really was, he thought. The rock walls dripped with moisture. Small lights embedded into the rock and the headlights of the truck illuminated the way. The walls were so close it felt like a person could reach an arm out each window and touch them. No matter how many times he'd been through, Annabeth was right, it was eerie.

Going the posted 25 mph speed limit and ignoring the SUV riding his bumper, it took seven minutes before they emerged into the town of Whittier. Population 300.

There wasn't really any way to get lost, but Cooper held his tongue when Annabeth pulled out a sheet of paper and started giving him directions to BTI, the residential building officially named Begich Tower Incorporated, after an Alaska congressman who was presumed killed in a plane crash in the area, though the wreckage had never been found. BTI housed nearly every Whittier resident.

They passed two large boat parking lots before pulling up to the building that, Cooper had decided when he was young, looked like a Lego house, a tri-colored rectangular box with rows of windows.

"Ready?" he asked Annabeth after finding a parking space near the front of the building.

"Yep," she said and was out the door before he had the chance to come around and open it for her.

Inside the building, they walked past the closed doors of several government offices, including that of the mayor, and the post office. The general store was still open with its few shelves of necessities like toilet paper, laundry detergent, candy, canned goods, boxed meals and such. Cooper caught a glimpse of the old-fashioned cash register where the amounts of each item popped up in the window. Nowadays, you'd expect to find something like that only in a museum.

As he expected, they found the building management office closed with a sign that said they'd open the following day at 9:00 a.m.

"It's okay," Cooper told Annabeth. "I sort of know my way. You said Maggie would be at the school."

"Sort of?" She raised a single eyebrow.

"Hmm, ninety percent." He walked across the hall from the management office and up a few steps, then poked the button to call the elevator.

The door opened immediately and he held it as she stepped in. Inside, he pushed the button to the basement. "Okay, eighty percent."

The elevator door opened to the bowels of the building. Again, Cooper held the door and waited for Annabeth to step out. Metal pipes ran like a city freeway overhead. In front of them, at least half the size of the whole building was a maze of chain-linked, padlocked cages that served as storage for the BTI residents.

"This way," he said, more confidently than he felt. The only sound was the thud of their steps on the cement floor and the buzz of the fluorescent lights above. Despite the lights, it still felt dark.

"This place has all the makings of a horror film," she said, and Cooper felt Annabeth take a step closer to him. Without thinking, he took her hand.

"Nobody lives in the other building, right?" she asked. He suspected she wanted the sound of her own voice to drown out the horror film light buzzing sound overhead. The other building was a copycat of BTI.

"Right. It's been abandoned as long as I can remember."

"It so strange the entire town lives in one building."

"No kidding. This was built during World War Two and the original plan was to build seven or nine buildings, depending on who you ask. This was before there was even a tunnel to get here. You got here on boats mostly."

"Why?" she asked.

"The idea was that if Anchorage had to be evacuated in the event of an attack, residents would come here. At the time, the buildings were going to be enough to hold every Anchoragite. But they never finished beyond the two. I'm not sure why. Maybe the war ended."

"Would make sense."

"Most people didn't, probably still don't, realize how much closer Asia is to Alaska than to other western states. After Pearl Harbor, Alaska seemed especially vulnerable, since it's closer to Japan than Hawaii. Another thing most people don't know is that, in fact, six months after Pearl Harbor, the Japanese bombed the two most western islands of Alaska at the end of the Aleutian chain. Alaska sourdoughs sometimes called it the Forgotten War, since no one seems to remember that campaign and subsequent takeover of the islands. A tiny bit of Alaska was actually occupied during the war. Of course, we weren't a state yet."

"Interesting."

"History major," he said, raising his hand. What was up with him tonight? Kind of a chatty Cathy. First about his childhood pets and now a history lesson. It was so unlike him. Or, so unlike the person he'd turned into in the last year. "I'm just trying to distract you from the fact that, really, it's probably about sixty percent."

She laughed out loud.

"Just kidding," he said a second later when they turned a corner and came to a set of tan double doors. "I knew where I was going all along."

"Ask me if I believe that."

He didn't want to drop her hand, but did to open the door. "Not going to do it," he said as she passed in front of him into the underground corridor.

The metal door closed with a hollow thud behind them. The temperature dropped by 20 degrees because they were really walking through an unheated tunnel carved in the rock just below ground level. Plywood walls were painted with a green and blue summer mountain scene by the children from the school they were walking toward.

"Why'd they build the tunnel?" Annabeth asked.

"Not sure. Maybe Alaska winters and the idea that it would be easier to get from building to building via tunnels, especially in the forties before big snow removal equipment. I'm pretty sure all seven or nine buildings were going to connect underground."

"Couldn't we just have driven to the school?" Annabeth asked.

"Hmm. Honestly, I didn't think of that. We are under the school's parking lot right now. Let's call it stupidity from lack of sleep."

"Genius," she teased.

"Actually, I'm guessing that at this hour, the doors outside into the school are probably locked."

"Nice save," she said and grabbed his arm.

Cooper's body unexpectedly reacted to her touch. It had been a long time since a woman had stirred him. More than a year. He wasn't sure if he liked that idea.

The corridor wasn't long, the length of a small parking lot. They reached the matching tan metal double doors opposite the set they had walked through from BTI. Cooper tugged on one of the handles.

But it was locked.

He pulled again but it didn't move. He tried the other door with the same result.

In that moment, behind them they heard a small but distinct sound of metal sliding into metal.

Annabeth spun around and ran back to the door they'd come through. She put a hand on each door handle and pulled. Nothing but the sound of the door giving the tiniest bit before stopping from a metal dead bolt. She pounded on the door. "Let us out."

Cooper tried both his doors again. Nothing.

He turned to face her as she did the same. She shrieked, "It's happening again."

Eight

At least no one was holding a gun on her. The situation wasn't as bad as it felt, Annabeth repeated to herself. The corridor was cold because it wasn't heated, but not so cold that they'd freeze to death. Today was Wednesday. Tomorrow was a school day, which meant the longest they'd be trapped was 12 hours. She just had to keep it together until the morning. Thankfully, they'd both used the restroom on the main level before heading down. She was scared, but not nearly as much as last night.

It was easy to think that, now that the panic of the moment had passed and she could look at the situation logically. It wasn't true an hour ago when they discovered they were locked in. First, they had tried to figure out a way to unlock the door. But with a deadbolt, which they could clearly make out between the sliver of space between the two doors on either end of the corridor, there was just no way.

She had pounded until the sides of her hands hurt. First on the set of doors to BTI. Then on the set of doors to the school. Then back again. And back again, hoping against hope they weren't trapped.

Their cell phones were useless. Whittier, with mountains on three sides, the bay to the ocean on the other, not to mention the wind and remoteness, got poor reception. Underground, it was nonexistent, no matter how many times they looked at their phones.

You only had to look around to see there was no ventilation in the tunnel and still the image of the corridor filling with a deadly gas was never far from her mind. Maybe this was about her, the person, after all. Did someone want her dead? Maybe last night and the gunman acting like she had something he wanted had been all a ruse. Maybe it was all just to get her into his car where he'd take her away. But why?

Eventually, her mind and body, beaten down to nothing, had just sunk to the hard floor and she began to weep. Instantly, Cooper was by her side. He put his arm around her, stroking her hair, uttering reassuring sounds until she was spent. She thought she'd gotten it all out when she'd cried in the drop-off area earlier in the day. But, nope, it turned out there was more inside.

If she hadn't been such a wreck, a shell, she might have pushed Cooper away. She hated feeling vulnerable and weak. At some point, he'd stuffed a white handkerchief into her hand. She didn't know men even carried those anymore. It made her think of her grandfather, the sweetest man she ever knew. He had died when Annabeth was still a child. Nevertheless, she had such clear memories of helping her grandmother iron and fold his snow-bleached handkerchiefs into perfect squares.

Once she calmed and her mind came back to itself, she realized Cooper was the light at the end of the tunnel, so to speak. She might truly have gone out of her own mind if she'd come to Whittier and ended up locked in this tunnel alone.

"Why is this happening?" she finally asked.

"I don't know," he said. "I've been asking myself what purpose is served by locking us in here? None that I can see. We're going to get out. I know it cannot possibly feel like it and I know you won't like hearing this, but I'm wondering if this is just a very weird, freakishly-timed coincidence. Maybe some kid is playing a prank or a maintenance person locked the doors not realizing we were in here."

"That'd be a mammoth-sized coincidence if it's true. You only have to watch one or two detective shows to know cops hate coincidences.

Don't believe in them." Annabeth wiped her face again, sopping up the last of the tears. She blew her nose. His poor handkerchief. It was never going to be the same.

"If not a coincidence, it would mean someone followed us here and I didn't notice anyone," he told her.

"What about the car that beeped at the entrance to the tunnel?"

"Think about it. If that SUV were following us, why beep and draw attention? I looked in the rear view mirror, I saw the guy's face."

He was probably right. "I'm so sorry," she finally said. "This is all my fault. If I hadn't insisted on coming tonight, we wouldn't be in this mess."

"It's not your fault. You didn't lock us in here. And you couldn't have known someone else would," he said, stroking her hair, which caused an unexpected tingly feeling down her spine. "You know what I don't get?" he said.

"Everything? All of it?" she almost laughed.

"Well, yeah, that. No, I mean, even if this isn't a coincidence and, somehow the tall man followed us and locked the door when we came into the tunnel from BTI—"

She suddenly knew exactly where he was going. Why hadn't either of them thought of it earlier? It didn't change anything, but still.

He finished, "—why is the door to the school also locked? Where's Maggie? She told us to come to the school, right?"

Annabeth went back to the hurried conversation she'd had with Maggie when she telephoned to ask to come out to see her. Maggie, understandably hesitant since Annabeth wouldn't tell her what it was about over the phone, said she'd be at the school. She'd volunteered to help her husband, the fourth and fifth grade teacher, organize his classroom for a project the kids were starting the next day.

Wait, she thought. Then said it out loud. "Wait. What she said was that they'd *probably* be at the school. I didn't even think about it. I should've called her before we went through the tunnel." Annabeth pulled her phone from her pocket and looked at the time. "How long have we been in here?"

"An hour or more, I'd guess," Cooper said.

"So, we got locked in about six forty-five?"

"We went through the tunnel at six-thirty. So, yeah, here after that. Why?"

"Just trying to remember exactly what she said. She gave me their condo number." She flipped through the notes section of her phone where she'd typed it. "Here. Seventh floor, condo seven-o-six." Annabeth closed her eyes, trying to replay the exact conversation. "She said, 'Come on over. We live in BTI seven-o-six, but we'll probably be across the way at the school.' Then she went on and on about helping her husband with his classroom. Honestly, I tuned it out a little because I was just thinking how glad I was she agreed to the visit. And I made a mental note to go to the school."

"So, that's it. At least for these doors." He leaned back and knocked his head against the metal door. "Ouch," he said and rubbed his hand over the back of his head. "That smarts."

Annabeth reach over and touched the back of his head. "Wow. You really do have a lump back here."

"You sound surprised," Cooper said.

"Yeah, I mean, no. I mean, I know you hit your head. I was there. I didn't realize how hard you hit it. I kind of saw you catch yourself a little as you went down."

"It was so fast I don't remember catching myself. But I do remember my head connecting with the floor. So, if they finished in the classroom, they had to have been the last people to leave the school, which means they're the ones who probably locked it."

"That would explain this set being locked," she said. "But not those." Annabeth pointed to the doors at the other end of the corridor.

As they sat with their backs against the door to the school, a quiet came over the weird cold tunnel with the summer sunshine mural painted on plywood. Annabeth felt heavy with equal parts exhaustion, frustration and fear.

She thought of suggesting they do more outside the box thinking, come up with more improbable theories. More rabbit holes and mind circles. At least it would keep them busy. After all, they had many hours to kill.

She wanted to believe it might help to forgot about their current circumstance and everything that led to it. But that was impossible to forget, no matter what they talked about. Her backside was going numb from sitting. Her thick winter coat did little to help because, even though the concrete floor was covered with a layer of carpet, it had no padding.

Instead of more theories, she surprised herself when she heard the words come out of her mouth. "Why aren't you married?"

He surprised her even more by retorting, "Why aren't you?"

"You know, the downside of being a new employee is not knowing co-workers' narratives. I don't know anyone's story yet." She shifted to get feeling into her behind, then said, "Besides, I asked you first."

"Okay, then," he finally answered. "I was married."

"What? Really?" she said. She felt, strangely, a little jealous. "Was?"

"She died. Car accident. Just a week before Thanksgiving, last year."

Annabeth expected a story of divorce. She wasn't prepared for death. "Oh, I'm so sorry. I had no idea. So young."

"Thanks. Yeah, too young. She was alone in the car."

Quiet settled around them again because, really, what could she say to that? It was natural to wonder about the details. She hated herself for her next thought, but she'd made a mental note to do an internet search for the details once they got out of this place.

"Actually, she wasn't alone," he said. "My dog—our dog—was with her. The one I told you about earlier. Scout."

She nodded.

"He didn't survive either. He might have, but she didn't have him secured. We used to fight about that all the time."

"That's horrible," she cried, a tad louder than she meant. "To lose two people you loved on the same day."

"It was hard. I was so angry for months afterward. People kept telling me it was normal, but what they didn't understand was that I was angry at her for killing Scout. But the hardest part—" he started.

"What?"

"The hardest part was the part I couldn't talk to anyone about. We married way too young and we were having problems when she died. Real problems. It's strange to say this. I grieved for her the way any husband would, but there were times I felt like a complete fraud."

"I don't get it. Why?" Annabeth asked.

"If she hadn't died, I know with one hundred percent certainty we wouldn't be together right now. We would've spent the holidays last year together just out of habit. But probably not Valentine's Day."

She wanted to say something to comfort him, but what did she know? She was the last person to offer comforting words about relationships. She said the only thing that came to mind. "That doesn't make you a fraud."

She knew by his silence what she offered was weak. Should she try to get him to talk more? Change the subject?

Before she could decide, he started talking again. "Then two months ago, my mom got sick—really sick, really fast. I went to see her thinking we—my brothers and I—would come up with a plan for taking care of her. We never made that plan because she died ten days later. Then there's so much to do after someone dies. Going through her stuff, executing her will, selling her house. I was numb. Still am, I suppose. But the whole time, I just kept thinking *I wish my wife were here*. The funny thing is she was a terrible person to have around in a crisis. Even so, problems or not, right or wrong, I just kept thinking I didn't want to be alone."

"That's understandable."

"Is it? I don't know." He looked far away, lost in memory. He shook his head as if to get the thoughts out of his mind and looked at her. "Why did I just tell you all that? One has nothing to do with the other. And none of that has to do with what's going on with us."

"With us?" Annabeth felt that little tingle again.

"Last night. The finances. This," he said hitting his head against the door again. "Damn it," he said, reaching up and rubbing his head again.

To avoid being asked why she wasn't married, she said, "Oh, I didn't ask. I forgot. What did the staff say about your email telling them what happened?"

Cooper chuckled. "You aren't going to believe this," he said, clearly glad to be on to another subject. "Shannon forwarded the email to all the volunteers and Ruthie—you know the Wednesday morning volunteer?"

"Yeah," Annabeth said. Ruthie was the one he'd been talking to when she had to duck into the drop-off room.

"She came into my office before she left for the day. She asked if she could talk to me. So I told her to sit down. I thought she was going to say how upsetting it was, or even that she no longer felt comfortable being at the front desk. Instead, she said she wanted to let me know she packs."

"What! As in a gun?"

"Yep. Her words: *she packs*. She said no hoodlum would be causing any ruckus during her shift. It took every bit of self-control I had to not laugh. You should've seen her. Just as serious as she could be. Like she was going to protect me from the bogeyman."

"Ruthie, a gun-toting white hair. You'd never know by looking at her."

"No, you wouldn't. Zoey and Shannon came in, too. Mostly they wanted to check on me. And you. They grilled me a little about what happened, asked if there was anything they could do. I repeated what I said in the email. Just keep an eye out."

"I hope no one else gets dragged into this," Annabeth said. She felt bad enough over Cooper getting caught up in the drama, first his head and face from the fight yesterday, and now getting him locked in a cold tunnel for the night.

~ * ~

Annabeth startled awake. Had she heard something? They must've fallen asleep. Her head, resting on Cooper's shoulder, was foggy. She was cold, stiff. What time was it?

Then she heard it again.

She shook Cooper awake. "Someone's here," she whispered and pointed to the doors on the other end, the doors from BTI.

Her mind sharpened and her senses alerted, she no longer felt the cold or stiffness. Being trapped, her body and mind had no choice. Flight wasn't an option. She prepared to scream on the off-chance someone might hear. Prepared to fight. It was two against one. Somewhere inside of her, she was even prepared to face the tall man and his gun.

What she wasn't prepared to do was to die.

Nine

Cooper woke, alert. Both he and Annabeth were on their feet in an instant. Cooper experienced a Twilight Zone *déjà vu* moment as he wished for a weapon, anything to protect them. He even wished for a binder filled with adoption certificates like the night before. He had nothing except his fists and his wits. They listened intently.

Cooper, operating only on instinct, grabbed Annabeth by the coat and pulled her toward him. And kissed her. Fast and furious, it was hard to call it a good kiss. It certainly wasn't a proper one. But he'd be damned if he'd die without having pressed his lips to another's in more than a year. Especially this woman.

They heard the distinct sound of metal in the lock. Then the sound of the deadbolt retracting. He watched as the handle rotated and the door slowly opened.

Before they could see who stood on the other side, Copper swept his arm in front of Annabeth and pushed her behind him. He'd do everything possible to shield her, to protect her, but he feared, in their current circumstances, it wouldn't be enough.

The door opened and Cooper almost couldn't comprehend what he saw, it being so different from what he was braced for. He blinked and stared.

Then he burst out laughing. He turned to face Annabeth, who'd stepped out from behind him. She was chuckling, her head shaking side to side.

"What are you doing in here? What's so funny?" the old man on the other end asked as he shuffled through the door, a carrier of cleaning supplies in hand.

Cooper and Annabeth walked toward the stooped man as he approached them. "We got locked in," Annabeth said.

"Locked in?" He regarded them skeptically.

Cooper explained how they heard the door lock as they were going through the tunnel only to find the school also locked.

"Well, I'll be," the man said. All three stopped when they met in the middle of the corridor just in front of the giant yellow sun on the mural. The man set the clear plastic carrier on the ground. "I don't believe I've ever known anyone to get locked in the tunnel. The BTI door wasn't supposed to be locked. It doesn't get locked until I finish cleaning the school at ten."

Annabeth thanked him, Cooper shook his hand and the man picked up his carrier and continued on. "You folks have a good evening," he said.

"You too," Cooper said. Before they left the corridor, Cooper turned one last time to see the man on the other end, his carrier on the ground again, as he pulled keys from his pocket and unlocked the door to the school.

After a needed stop at the restrooms, Cooper led Annabeth back through the maze of chain-link storage units toward the elevator. He pushed the button and heard the wind of the elevator as it descended from above.

"How do you feel?" he asked. He wasn't entirely sure if he was asking in reference to getting locked in the tunnel and being rescued by the janitor. Or the kiss.

"I overreacted," she said. "You were right. There's no way we were followed here. It's unlikely the guy with the gun is the person who locked the door. I feel so stupid."

"It was a heightened reaction in a heightened situation. We didn't know it was the janitor who'd be coming through that door."

The elevator arrived. Inside, Cooper watched as Annabeth hesitated, then pressed the button for the seventh floor.

"So stupid," she repeated. "The screaming. The crying."

"Don't worry about it. It's okay. You've been through a lot in the last twenty-four hours." He had the strongest urge to reach out and take her in his arms, to reassure her once again.

She continued as if she hadn't heard him, looking up, watching the buttons of each floor light up as they passed. "I don't know. This whole goose chase is probably for nothing. Maybe we should just head back to Anchorage. I'll check into a hotel for a few days. I doubt Maggie will be of any help."

"We're here. We came all this way. Let's talk to her. Think outside the box, remember?"

Annabeth's face was stoic. He ached for her, her fear. She just looked so defeated. No matter the outcome of getting locked in the tunnel, it didn't change last night and the fact that they still had no idea what the man had been after. And, more importantly, it didn't change the uncertainty of whether the scumbag would be back. Kissing her had probably only made things worse.

A large plastic wreath covered in red bows adorned Maggie's front door. Various cat cutouts in Santa hats covered the bottom half. "'Tis the season," Cooper said, trying to lighten the mood before knocking.

Maggie opened her front door and greeted them warmly, pulling each into her soft fleshy arms. First Cooper. Then Annabeth. Somehow, Maggie seemed to know Annabeth needed an especially long embrace.

"What happened?" she said to Cooper when they stepped into the entryway of the condo with enough light for her to get a better look at his face, touching her own cheek.

"It's nothing," Cooper said.

"Well, come in," Maggie said, then pointed to the row of hooks along the entryway wall. "You can hang your coats there."

Inside, Maggie introduced Annabeth to her husband, Joe.

"Nice to see you again," Cooper said to the older man. Cooper had met Joe many times over the years at company Christmas parties and a plethora of Rescued Paws' fundraising events. He wasn't much of a talker but always struck Cooper as a decent guy.

To explain their tardiness, Cooper relayed the story of getting locked in the tunnel, but called it an accident and omitted the screaming, crying and kissing from his story.

"Oh dear," Maggie said, then repeated what the janitor had said about never having heard of that happening.

The pleasantries behind them, Joe excused himself. "His programs," Maggie leaned over and whispered after he'd left to another room where they heard a television click on.

Maggie instructed Cooper and Annabeth to make themselves at home in the living room while she prepared tea. Two days in a row he'd been offered tea. That was certainly a first.

Annabeth sat on the blue and green paisley couch while Cooper took a seat across from her on an overstuffed navy blue chair. They hadn't really talked about a strategy for this meeting. How do you ask the former employee about the finances during her reign without sounding accusatory?

"You okay?" he whispered.

"I'm fine. Sorry."

"Stop apologizing," he said. "So how do we do this? Do we tell her about last night?"

Annabeth tilted her head in thought. It was obvious she hadn't thought about how to approach the subject either. "I'm not sure. We almost have to, right? Otherwise, how can we ask if she knows anything? And the cat's halfway out of the bag, anyway, with that bruise on your face."

"Good point." Before he could ask who should do the talking, Maggie came into the room with a tray. As she approached, Cooper could smell the tea, but what he saw was the plate of cookies. He loved Maggie's cookies. And since it was the second night in a row that the dinner hour had passed without food, they were especially welcomed.

Annabeth leaned forward to push aside the large picture book of Alaska's Mount Denali to make room for Maggie to set the tray on the coffee table.

"Thanks, dear," Maggie said. She handed a cup and saucer to Annabeth. Then one to Cooper. "That's coffee," she said to him. "I know you aren't a tea kind of guy."

"Perfection. Thanks, Mag."

"And both of you help yourself to cookies. I made them this morning."

Maggie took her tea cup then sat near Annabeth on the couch. "And if either of you needs a little nip, I brought this." She pulled a small flask from the pocket of her oversized sweater. "Whiskey."

"Maggie!" Cooper feigned astonishment.

"You're not my boss anymore," she teased back. "You can't tell me what to do. Besides, it's how I keep my youthful complexion and get a good night's sleep. A little nip of this with my evening tea and I sleep right through Joe's snoring. I adore that man, but he could wake the dead." She laughed.

Cooper offered his cup across the table and waited for Maggie to pour in a nip.

Annabeth, too, graciously accepted a nip.

Cooper noticed that Maggie poured herself a double nip.

"Okay," she said after the silver flask found its way back into her deep pocket. "What's this all about?"

Cooper looked to Annabeth, who looked back to him. She pointed her chin in his direction, indicating she wanted him to tell the story.

He tried to be as succinct and G-rated as possible, but it was hard, considering the story included a gun, a fistfight and the police. It was hard to dilute the story and still impress upon her the urgency of the situation.

Maggie's response throughout was whispered. There was one, "Oh my," and several, "Oh, honey," directed to Cooper when he shared the fight. And at the end she said, "I'm so sorry that happened to you two but glad you're okay."

"Us too," Cooper said, taking two cookies.

"But I'm still not sure why you wanted to see me," Maggie said.

"I know it's confusing," Annabeth cut in. "We are going crazy trying to figure this out. And since I'm new, we thought maybe you'd have some idea what he might've been looking for. Or what he wanted."

"Me?" she said, horrified. "No, of course not."

"We knew you probably didn't. But, like I said, since I'm new and Cooper's been gone, we wanted to ask, because neither us has a clue what he was after."

Maggie thought a minute then shook her head. "Nope. I cannot think of a single reason."

"Does 'certified' mean anything?" Annabeth asked. "I swear he said something about something being certified."

"Like what he was looking for was certified?" Maggie asked.

"Maybe. It's not clear in my mind, so it also might not have been certified, but I can't think of other things that would be close to that word."

Cooper watched Maggie wrack her memory. "The only thing that even remotely comes to mind is certified mail. I doubt that can be it, though. You know this, Annabeth, from our training. The only stuff we send certified mail are government documents like quarterly payroll tax reports, which won't be due until January. That, and grant reports. Random stuff comes into the office certified mail, but that's very little and very infrequently. None of it is sent with money. That's all electronic these days."

"True," Annabeth confirmed.

"Certified. Certified. Hmm?" Maggie continued thinking aloud. "Nothing even sounds like it. Certified. Fried? Spied? Tried? Died? No, that can't be it." She withdrew the flask from her pocket again. "Another nip? Cooper? Annabeth? Might help the old gray matter," she said, tapping the end of it to the side of her head.

They both declined. Maggie continued to mouth the word 'certified' as she unscrewed the cap and poured another double nip into her cup before once again returning the flask to her sweater's pocket. "I don't know if this really sounds the same. Maybe certificates? Like the adoption certificates or the certificates of appreciation we give to volunteers? No, that's dumb."

Cooper couldn't make heads or tails of it, and, like when Annabeth had remembered it earlier in the day, he was inclined to think she'd misheard or misremembered. "The other thing Annabeth remembered hearing him say was 'money.' Does that mean anything?"

"Money?"

"Yeah, and he didn't demand her purse or petty cash or anything obvious like that, so we don't think it was about robbery," Cooper offered.

Annabeth jumped in to add an abbreviated version of their theory that it had something to do with the finances, but said she didn't find any obvious anomalies in the financials. Annabeth then went on to go through their ideas with Maggie. They covered what she'd told him about earlier during their meeting. New vendors. Invoices that might not have seemed quite right.

Cooper listened but only half understood the technical parts of their conversation.

But, in the end, Maggie's twenty years resulted in the same thing Annabeth's two hours had. Nothing.

The clock hanging on the wall, surrounded by way too many framed family photos, chimed. They'd been talking nearly an hour and now it was 8:30. As the conversation slowed, so did Cooper's attention. He desperately needed a good night's sleep and they still had an hour's drive back to Anchorage.

"Cooper?" Annabeth said, bringing him back.

"Sorry, I didn't hear."

Annabeth cocked her head toward Maggie.

"I asked how you and your brothers are doing," Maggie repeated. "You left the office so fast I never had the chance to tell you how sorry I was. Then I was gone by the time I'd heard your mother had passed. I sent a card."

He'd be going along fine and then he'd think of his mother, and grief hit him like a tsunami, but he didn't want to share the depth of his grief. "I'm sure I got it. Thank you. I guess the part of the story I didn't tell you was that yesterday was my first day back in the office. I flew back to town on Monday evening, so I haven't had the chance to read my mail. But I appreciate it, Maggie. I really do."

"If there's anything I can do…" she started.

"Thank you," he said again. He never knew what to say when people made the offer because what he wanted was his mother not to have died. And no one could do anything about that.

"Maybe a batch of cookies now and again?" she suggested.

"Oh, Mag, that would be perfect. But we probably need to get going."

"Let me just give you a few for the road." She got up and went to the kitchen while he and Annabeth rose and walked to the front door.

Cooper took Annabeth's coat from the hook and held it for her. She gave him her sweet smile as a way of saying thanks and touched his hand as he gripped the coat. He let his hand linger longer than was needed to help her on with it.

Maggie returned with a paper bag she handed to Annabeth while he shrugged on his own coat. This time it was his turn for the extra-long hug from Maggie as they said their goodbyes.

They promised to keep her updated. And then they were alone again in the poorly lit hallway.

Halfway to the elevator, Cooper heard a door open behind them. He turned to see Maggie emerging.

"Wait," she called. When she reached the pair she said, "Now, I'm sure it's nothing. I didn't think of it before but, you know, just in case. I did notice a decrease in pet adoptions starting about three years ago."

Ten

Thankfully, Maggie retreated from the hallway as quickly as she'd entered it after another goodbye. Remembering adoptions being down, Annabeth assumed, was a product of the whiskey more than relevant information.

At the elevator, Cooper said, tapping on his wrist, "We can talk about everything on the way back but right now we need to get to the tunnel. Pronto."

Annabeth retrieved her phone from her coat pocket and looked at the time, ten minutes until 9:00. The tunnel from this side opened on the hour and would stay open for five minutes. That meant if they didn't reach it by 9:05, they'd have to wait an entire hour for the last tunnel opening of the day. After that, they were just out of luck.

The prospect of sitting an extra hour in the truck with Cooper wasn't entirely unpleasant, though it wouldn't take long to cover everything they'd learned from this trip to Whittier. If it weren't a goose chase, it was about as close as you could get to one. What they'd learned, for all intents and purposes, was nothing. Well, not nothing. They learned Maggie liked whiskey.

But that didn't mean they couldn't go through everything again. They could talk through more possibilities.

But really, as they rode the elevator to the ground floor, Annabeth found herself wanting to find out more about Cooper. More than that, she wanted to discover why he'd kissed her in the tunnel. It was so fast and furious, she almost felt cheated. On the other hand, the last thing she needed was a great kiss from her new boss because that would make her want another. And another.

Stop, she scolded herself. *Pretend that kiss never happened*. That was the smart thing to do if she did not want to put herself into the position of needing to leave another job.

In the truck, Cooper didn't wait for the engine to warm. Its frozen metal car parts whined in protest as he sped out of the parking lot toward the tunnel. He barely did a rolling pause through the stop sign at the railroad crossing.

"I think we're going to make it," Annabeth said, the light from her phone illuminating the inside of the truck. "It's nine-o-three." They were still a mile away but it was straight in front of them and there was nothing in between.

"Great," Cooper said. "We don't have to stop because the fee is only charged on the way into Whittier."

Annabeth concentrated her attention between her phone and the tunnel lights in the distance. So much so, she didn't bother to read the flashing LED sign on the side of the road until they were right in front of it.

"Come on," Cooper said, slowing the truck to a stop when he saw it. He hit the steering wheel in frustration.

The sign informed them the tunnel had closed at 8:30 for scheduled maintenance and wouldn't be open until morning.

"This can't be happening." Cooper pointed out the windshield at a man with a reflective vest. "I'll be right back," he said.

Annabeth watched as Cooper walked over to the man. As near as she could tell, Cooper wasn't yelling at the guy and he wasn't wildly gesturing his frustration. Not that he struck her as the kind of guy who did either.

Cooper reached out and shook the guy's hand. Surely that was a good sign, Annabeth thought hopefully. She hadn't realized she was holding her breath. They needed out of this town tonight. This was Whittier. If you didn't live here, it was not an overnight kind of town. No hotels. No gas stations. That was true even in the summer at the height of tourist season.

The truck's interior light went on when Cooper opened the door. He got in but didn't shut the door.

"No luck," he said.

"No?"

"He said he'd let us through if he could, but they have a big piece of equipment in the middle of the tunnel at the moment. And all night. We're stuck here until the first opening tomorrow at seven."

"They should've told us that on the way in."

"I said the same thing. The guy said there is a sign just like this one on the other end."

"Really? I never saw it."

"That's what I said. He swore it's there. He also said we should've been told on the way in."

"Now the attendant definitely didn't tell us anything," Annabeth said. She felt fluttery and dizzy. They just had to get out of Whittier tonight.

Cooper dug the receipt from his cup holder along with the information sheet. He looked at both. He hit the steering wheel again in frustration, though not as hard as the first time.

He handed the larger piece of paper out for Annabeth. So it turned out they had been informed.

He shut the door and the truck light went out.

"Wouldn't the laws of probability suggest that, at some point, something has to go our way? Why is this so hard?" Annabeth asked.

"I don't know. Going with probability, let's look on the bright side, and take this as a sign that tomorrow will be better. Maybe we'll even figure everything out."

"It seems like wishful thinking, but I do like your optimism. So now what?"

"There aren't a lot of options," Cooper said.

"No kidding. We could stay right here. Try to get some sleep. Your truck is pretty comfortable," Annabeth suggested though it sounded like a terribly uncomfortable option.

Cooper shook his head. "Too cold, and I don't have enough gas for us to keep it running through the night and get us back to town."

"Back to Maggie's? Though I hate to impose on her like that. Not to mention, what if her evening nips have already kicked in? Sounded like they take her down for the count."

Cooper laughed. "I worked with her all those years and never knew about her nips. Why don't we save that as a last resort?"

"Last resort? I figured it was the only resort. What other option is there?"

"There is a B&B that opened a couple summers ago. One of the very few places not in BTI. Let's go see if they have two rooms." Cooper put the truck into drive, did a U-turn and headed back on the same road. The only road. This time minding the speed limit.

"Do you think they'll even be open for business during the winter?" Annabeth asked, fearing that no matter how he answered, the real answer was probably no.

The good, albeit surprising, news was they were open. The bad news was—unbelievable as this was in the middle of December—they only had one room available. The other three rooms were filled with the bride's family, they were told. A weekend wedding of a local boy, according to the proprietor, who insisted they call her Mrs. B. Mrs. B of Mrs. B's B&B. Silly or cute? Annabeth couldn't decide. When Cooper asked if there were any other options, Mrs. B's jovial laugh was her answer.

Annabeth tried to keep cool when Cooper suggested it was a better option than going back to Maggie's. Still, she felt heat rising to her face.

"It'll be fine. We'll make the best of it and get back to town first thing in the morning."

When stuck in Whittier, what else could she do but agree with a smile?

"Look on the bright side," he said as Mrs. B walked away with his credit card. "If we can't get out of town, it also means the bad guy can't get in. Should ease your mind. Maybe make for a good night's sleep."

It was hard holding a straight face and agreeing to that one. With him only feet away, a good night's sleep was the last thing she expected.

Mrs. B returned with a receipt for Cooper to sign. Then he told Annabeth he'd catch up with her as he needed a few things from the truck.

Mrs. B was a slight, dark-haired woman in need of a touchup on her hair color, Annabeth noticed as she followed her to the lone available room.

Rough wood walls gave the room the appearance of a cozy rustic cabin. A double bed with a fluffy brown duvet was near one of the walls to allow space for a small sitting area with a love seat, a chair with matching foot stool and a television, mounted unusually low on the wall.

The owner saw her looking at it and explained, "It's not a tv. Everyone thinks it is. It's a fireplace." Mrs. B picked up the remote from a little side table and pushed a button. A roaring fire appeared. "For the full cabin effect," she said, clicking it back off and setting the remote down.

"Thanks," Annabeth said. She was glad Mrs. B had turned it off. Annabeth didn't want this place to feel any more romantic or cozy than it already did. "Could we get an extra blanket and pillow? I'll sleep on the loveseat. I'll be like Goldilocks, it's just my size."

"This never happens in the winter months," Mrs. B apologized again. Of course it doesn't, Annabeth thought sarcastically. "I'll get you the extra linens."

A few minutes later, Annabeth heard a light knock, and the door opened. Cooper stood in the doorway loaded down. Mrs. B had obviously intercepted him on his way to the room. In addition to a duffel bag slung on each arm, he held the stack of bedding.

Annabeth grabbed the bedding while he dropped the bags. She set it on the bed as Cooper took off his coat and brought the red duffel over to the sitting area. "I have something to show you," he said with a mischievous smile.

She had no idea what it could be.

He moved the duffel up to the footstool and Annabeth sat on the chair. He unzipped the duffel, whipped it open and announced, "Dinner."

Since Maggie's, Annabeth had been trying to ignore the hunger pangs. At least they hadn't embarrassingly tried to announce themselves like Cooper had the night before. "This is great," Annabeth reached in and sifted through his booty. She found bags of dried fruit and granola, a can of raw almonds and another of roasted cashews, a box of crackers, nutrition bars, chocolate bars, and several backpacker meals-in-a-bag. "May I?" she asked.

"Help yourself. There's a stove and a gas can there, too. Let me start boiling water and we'll make up a couple of the meals." Annabeth opened a bag of trail mix, cupped her hand and filled it. Sweet and salty, it tasted so good.

While he got water from the bathroom, Annabeth looked at the meals and found a tofu and vegetable stew that looked delicious, if the picture on the front was any indication.

Annabeth had never backpacked, so was fascinated to watch as Cooper attached the tiny stove that, to her eye, looked like bent paperclips, to a very small orange gas can and lit it. He carefully set his gray metal pot on the stove.

"It's fast," he assured her. He looked through the bag and selected his meal-in-a-bag, a macaroni chili cheese dinner. Then he opened the can of cashews.

"Is this your emergency kit?" Every Alaskan knew to have emergency supplies in their vehicle, especially during the winter months.

"Part of it. This is the food. Obviously."

"It makes my blanket, boots and box of granola bars looks pretty wimpy," she said and poured a few cashews into her hand.

"That's all you have?"

"Well, I also have the important stuff like an emergency car kit with those orange triangles, flares, and a first aid kit."

"Those are good, but you really should carry more food and definitely more than one blanket. One blanket won't save you from freezing on a really cold night. I'm going to make you a proper Alaska emergency car kit. Water's boiling. Hand me your dinner." Annabeth opened the top of her stew and held open the foil package while Cooper poured the boiling water in. He took the package from her and set it on the carpet, stirred the contents then sealed it for cooking.

His pot only held enough water for one package, so he returned to the bathroom to fill the pot again.

"You know if you do make me a kit, you'll also have to teach me how to use that thing," Annabeth said, pointing to the paperclip stove.

"Deal," he said. "Why is that tv so low?" He seemed to have noticed it for the first time.

Annabeth hoped he wouldn't ask. It was bad enough they were going to be spending the night in the same room. Fake or not, she really didn't want to tell him it wasn't a television. But she also didn't want to lie. She picked up the remote and clicked it on just as the owner had shown her.

"Wow," he said. The water started to boil a second time. Like the first, Annabeth opened his pouch and held it open while he poured. "It's just like we're camping. We'll pretend we boiled the water over a roaring crackling fire."

The sight and sound of the faux fire was nice. She could admit that.

Cooper went back to the bathroom and returned with two plastic cups filled with water while Annabeth dug through the bag to retrieve the crackers to go with her stew, and two spoons. And a few minutes later, dinner was served.

It was delicious. Surprisingly so, considering it was from a bag that had been in another bag in Cooper's truck for who knew how long. Maybe it was the fact that she was so hungry. Or, maybe it was because she couldn't stop thinking about the two of them out in the wilderness camping.

Cleanup involved tossing the empty food pouches and returning the stove to the duffel. That was her kind of cleanup. They both wished they had thought to bring in the paper bag of Maggie's cookies, but neither wanted to venture back out in the cold. Instead, they shared a bar of chocolate and some dried fruit for dessert.

After they were happily full, they settled back in their seats. "I guess we should get some sleep," Cooper said, though it sounded more like a question than a statement.

"I feel like we've been avoiding talking about our meeting with Maggie," Annabeth said. *And the kiss,* she thought but couldn't bring herself to say aloud.

"Yeah. It was nice to forget about that whole mess for a bit."

"I know. Thanks for dinner, by the way. It hit the spot."

"Anytime. We'll have plenty of time to talk on the drive tomorrow. About Maggie and how little we learned." He smiled, waited a beat, then added, "Then, should we talk about the kiss? Do I need to apologize?"

Annabeth froze. She'd hoped they'd both chalked it up to the situation, could pretend it hadn't happened. She absolutely did not want to talk about the kiss. She especially didn't want to talk about it here alone in a room with a roaring fire. And a bed.

One thing she heard loud and clear during their time in the tunnel was that he didn't want to be alone which, as Annabeth learned the hard way—the oh, so hard way—was the worst reason to start a relationship. She thought, for the tenth or twentieth time since she'd met him—what?—only 27 hours earlier, he was her boss. An even more painful lesson she'd learned was that an affair with the boss, no matter how discreet you thought you were being, would be found out. What followed—the shame, embarrassment, whispers and shift in the way co-workers treated her—had resulted in Annabeth leaving a job she liked very much.

Two excellent reasons for her to immediately shut down this attraction she felt for Cooper.

When she let too much silence hang in the air, Cooper nervously added, "Yeah, I need to apologize. And I do. I know it was inappropriate and pretty terrible on top of that."

Without thinking she said, "It wasn't terrible." What had she just decided? So, she added, "Just too fast to be memorable." She half suspected she was trying to convince herself rather than him that she wouldn't remember the kiss.

A surprised look crossed his face, but he recovered quickly. She could tell her words stung and that hadn't been her intention. She didn't want to be harsh with him, but it was vital for her to remember what was important. The priority was to keep the job, to not be attracted to her boss, to any boss, for the rest of her working life. Annabeth looked into his dark eyes, a tiny flicker of light dancing in them from the glow of the fake fire. Still, she couldn't bring herself to let his feelings be hurt. "I didn't mean that," she said. "I mean, I meant it. The kiss was fast. It wasn't terrible. But—"

Before she could finish her thought, he cut her off. "We could fix that. The memorable part. The fast part. Right here. Right now. Let me try again," he said.

"Cooper," she said, her resolve weakening only seconds after making the resolution. He was athletic, kind, caring. Her own age. Everything her previous boss was not. Not true, her previous boss had been caring and kind. "We cannot," she said simply and quietly.

He surprised her by jumping up with an, "Okay then." He stepped across the room and grabbed the blue duffel from the floor where he'd dropped it. "Gym bag," he said. "I think there might be something in here for each of us to sleep in."

Annabeth used the opportunity to turn off the fire. Her head was spinning. He recovered so quickly from her rejection. Most men would resort to begging or pouting. Or getting really nasty. She went to where he had opened the bag on the bed.

"Here we go," he said, as he pulled a t-shirt from the bag. "I think this'll work for you. And I have a pair of sweatpants I can wear."

He handed her the t-shirt. "Thank you," she said. She hadn't even thought about what they might wear to bed. And this was so much better than her clothes, since wearing nothing wasn't an option. She looked at the sweatpants in his hand and told herself she wasn't allowed to look at him in them, presumably without a shirt.

"It's lucky timing. I washed everything two months ago, but then with the leave, I haven't been back to the gym since."

"Lucky," she agreed. "I'll go change."

When she reached the bathroom, she heard, "And Annabeth?" She turned around, his back toward her as he continued to look through the duffel.

"Yeah?" she asked.

"If you change your mind. I'd really like the chance to do it again. I promise, it will be memorable."

Eleven

In the light of day—figuratively speaking, since Alaska's light of day in December wouldn't even consider peeking its head over the horizon for a couple more hours—Cooper felt foolish. There were a dozen things he should have done differently the day before, a dozen things he should have said differently.

He looked over at Annabeth in the passenger seat, her hands cupped around the large coffee Mrs. B had made each of them for the drive back to town. What was she thinking, he wondered. He found her hard to read, and reading people was something Cooper normally did with ease.

They were fifth in line at the tunnel. White exhaust from the line of cars curled up around them in the cold morning. Big pieces of equipment from the night's maintenance work were off to the side of the road. They still had another five or so minutes before the second tunnel opening, since they had missed the first one as they'd planned. Neither of them thought to set an alarm and, no doubt part of the reason they overslept was that they were both so tired.

Between the stress and then staying up late last night, Cooper didn't stir until he heard voices from the kitchen at the B&B. He wished sleep had come easily last night, but it hadn't, especially after seeing Annabeth in his college t-shirt. The faded old thing had never looked so good. It took more than an hour before he fell asleep.

Then, when he woke, he was stiff and sore. Two nights in a row on a couch were too much for his aging body. He wasn't the college kid of a decade earlier, where no matter what he did or didn't do the night before, the next morning he'd be fresh as a morning flower. When had he gone from that to a guy with lower back problems? Thirty-three wasn't *that* old.

He had found her reaction to his insistence that he sleep on the couch puzzling. No question, she'd fit much better on the short thing. Curled up, she might even find it comfortable. But there had been no way he would let a woman sleep on the couch while he took the bed. Why was she surprised by a man being a gentleman? Lack of experience with decent men? Is that why she was so guarded?

Or was it all in his head? Maybe he was projecting what he hoped explained her reaction. He was attracted to her. No denying that. But he'd been out of the new relationship game a long time—more than a decade—so he had to admit it was possible he completely misread the situation. He thought he'd picked up on her attraction to him but, clearly, she wasn't interested.

And if that weren't enough to make him feel foolish, remembering all he'd confessed to her while they were stuck between BTI and the school made him feel even worse. What made him think it was a good idea to talk about his marriage, his mother, his pain? He needed to find a way to process the last year of his life in a way that didn't involve telling an employee he barely knew his whole life story.

He heard Annabeth clear her throat, which brought him back to the present. "I have to say, I'm kind of glad we overslept," she said.

"Oh?"

"Those blueberry pancakes Mrs. B made were incredible. I cannot even remember the last time I had blueberry pancakes—or any pancakes—that delicious. I think they might just be the best pancakes I've had. Ever."

Cooper made a pretty mean pancake himself, but Annabeth was right. Mrs. B's were on a whole other level. "Agreed. I think her secret was the tart Alaska wild blueberries combined with the sweet homemade raspberry syrup."

"If I ever decided to pick Alaska berries, I'm not sure I'd be so willing to share them with strangers."

"If she serves those year-round, that's a whole lot of berry picking. Whoa. Wait. What do you mean if you ever decided to pick berries? You mean, you haven't? What kind of Alaskan are you?"

"I know. Every August I mean to and then I don't."

"Okay, so in addition to making you an emergency kit, I'm taking you berry picking next summer. I have a secret spot."

Annabeth laughed out loud. "Every Alaskan has a secret berry picking spot. Do you know how many times I've heard that?"

"But I really do," Cooper insisted. He loved hearing her laugh. He loved making her laugh.

The light on a wire over their lane changed from red to green. The line of cars shifted into drive and slowly moved forward. He assumed the handful of cars both in front of and behind them were commuters and he couldn't imagine doing this back and forth, day in and day out.

Once they made it back to the highway, it was time to start shifting back to reality. He hadn't heard anything that sounded like a lead from their interview with Maggie, but he hoped Annabeth had.

"Did anything click or red flag for you during our time with Maggie?" he asked.

Annabeth upended her paper cup to get the last of the coffee, then set it in the cup holder. "I wish it had," she said. "I'm still thinking it would be worth a few hours of my time to verify vendors, especially the ones who are newer and the ones with the largest invoices, but I didn't hear anything to explain what that guy was looking for."

"That's what I thought, too."

"Can I ask you something?"

"You can." Cooper wondered what it might be.

"If this crosses a line, let me know. You don't have to answer."

Now he was curious.

"Is Maggie really an accountant?"

He expected she wanted to know more about his personal life, so it took a second to wrap his head around the question, even though he understood it perfectly.

When he didn't answer right away, Annabeth added. "It doesn't matter. You don't have to answer if it's considered personal and none of my business. I was just wondering, because the way she talked about a few things—I don't know—it was just—how do I say this? Not accountant-like?"

Their conversation had sounded accountant-like to him, but what did he know? Cooper wasn't sure why, but he felt the need to defend Maggie. "Did you know Maggie was part of Rescued Paws when it started? She was a volunteer at first before they could even pay her. The company sent her to classes and found mentors to increase her knowledge to do the job. So, no, she's not an accountant."

"I wasn't judging, I promise. Just asking."

"What are you saying?"

"I'm not sure. I think what I'm saying is that if something were going on financially—and at this point that remains a big if—and if it were possible to spot—another big if—I just wonder if she'd have been able to spot it. I promise, I say this without judgment. You know, yesterday, I focused on the last five years. If someone were in it for the long game, maybe something has been going on for years. So many years that everything appears normal, especially when doing comparisons to years past."

"But who? How? Maggie was the longest employee. Board members turn over at least every ten years. I just don't see it. Not that I've seen how a financial crime was possible, since we started talking about this yesterday."

Annabeth didn't reply for a long time. "Yeah, that's the thing, isn't it?" she finally admitted. "Like I said, very big ifs. I know it may not have sounded like it, but I'm actually at the same place you are. I just don't see how anyone could be taking money from Paws. I'll still do some checks, but I don't think it's going to lead anywhere. And, yet, I can hear it so clearly in my mind when the guy said something about money but he didn't demand my purse or cash that Paws might have had on hand."

"What other kind of money is there?"

"I know. That's my point. What could he possibly have been talking about?"

Cooper concentrated as he passed a semi-truck on the two-lane highway before he admitted, "I'm out of ideas."

"Wait," Annabeth said. "Wait, wait. I feel like there is something on the edge of my brain. A thought. An idea. What is it?" Cooper stayed quiet while Annabeth dug around in her gray matter trying to retrieve the idea. "You know," she finally said as they came to the outskirts of town. Cooper reduced his speed. "We keep asking who and why. Who is this guy with the gun? What was he looking for? What does 'money' mean? What does 'certified' refer to? Basically, why did he come to Paws two nights ago."

"Right," Cooper agreed.

"Maybe we're asking the wrong questions," she said.

Cooper turned off the highway and headed toward their office. "What do you mean? What other questions are there?"

"I mean, we are asking why. Maybe we should ask why now?"

"Hmm," Cooper thought about that. "What about two nights ago?"

"Nothing comes to mind specifically about two nights ago, but in that general timeframe, Maggie had just left. I know we went over this yesterday and thought the guy might not have known I was new, because we thought he thought I might know what the heck he was talking about. But what if he came *because* I was new?"

"Okay."

"The other thing generally going now is you coming back."

"Me?"

"After having been gone for two months," she stated. "Maybe he didn't know you were back, which would explain why he didn't go to your office."

That felt like a bigger deeper rabbit hole than the one they'd travelled yesterday, but Cooper didn't want to stifle her outside-the-box thinking.

"I'm going to have to think on this more. There might be something there," she said.

Cooper pulled into Rescued Paws' parking lot, pulled around to the back of the building to employee parking. Three people had beat them to the office and, of course, the fourth car in the lot was Annabeth's, as it had never left.

After he parked, Annabeth jumped out and walked around to his side of the truck. He got out with their empty coffee cups in hand and locked the doors with his key fob.

"I hope no one sees us. Someone might get the wrong idea," she said.

"We'll just tell them you had a dead battery last night, so I gave you a ride," he said. It was an easy cover since once, last year, it had happened to him, and another employee had to give him a ride home then pick him up the next morning. Hopefully, no one remembered how, after that experience, he announced he would never take the jumper cables out of his truck again.

"Or that we are wearing the same clothes." She gave a little laugh. "It is kind of funny. At least we got sleep last night and showers this morning."

"Considering, I'd say we look pretty good," Cooper added. He was puzzled she hadn't started walking toward the building. It was as if she were stalling, and he couldn't figure out why.

Suddenly, she reached out and wrapped her arms around his waist. It was so sudden he didn't even have time to hug her back. "I just wanted to say thanks," she said. "For everything."

He smiled. "You don't have to thank me."

"Are you kidding? Where do I start? You probably saved my life. You took me to Whittier. You made me a pretend campfire dinner. Gave me the bed. Sincerely, thank you."

"You're sincerely welcome," he said simply.

Inside, they said goodbye and agreed to check back in with each other after lunch, if not before.

At his office, he found the message light on his phone blinking. No surprise. He was eight weeks behind. It was going to be a while before he was caught up with everything and everyone.

He got settled and started in on one of the many piles on his desk.

An hour later, the door to his office opened. He looked up and saw Annabeth standing in the doorframe. He couldn't read her but her face was serious. Was she pale? He felt the hair prickle on the back of his neck. He braced for what was to come.

She took a single step into his office, her head shaking, "You aren't going to believe this."

Twelve

Despite the cold and the urge to go inside where it was warm, Annabeth had found it hard not to linger as she hugged Cooper. But that was a bad idea and not just because they were standing in the employee parking lot. Maybe she shouldn't have done it to begin with, but she experienced a moment of utter gratitude toward Cooper, and she just didn't know how to adequately thank him for everything he'd done for her.

Inside the building, they had parted ways at the T-end of the hallway. Annabeth went to her office as Cooper headed to his. In her office, she dropped her bag, took off her coat, and headed toward the kitchen. Even though she'd had a cup of coffee with those amazing pancakes and another on the drive back, today felt like a three-cup day.

At the intake desk, she stopped and said hello to the Thursday morning volunteer, Stanley. He was a talker, so it took a few minutes to extricate herself to get to the kitchen.

Surprisingly, she had slept well the night before. Even so, she didn't feel quite ready to dive into the finances. She had a few current things to complete, but planned on spending most of her time researching their vendors and old invoices. She also decided to take another look for any financial anomalies, even though she'd done that very same thing yesterday. A second look with fresh eyes might uncover something new, even though she felt 99% sure there was nothing fishy going on, and whatever the gunman meant when he talked money, it wasn't Paws' money he was referring to.

In other words, most of today was probably going to be a big waste of time.

After she filled her mug, Annabeth headed to the warehouse. She decided she could afford a few minutes to visit Solstice. Coffee and puppy kisses. Then she'd be ready to tackle what lay ahead of her.

But in the warehouse, she found no Solstice. In fact, there were no dogs at all. Just a few cats, all napping.

In the lobby, Shannon leaned on the intake desk listening to Stanley retell the story he'd told her minutes earlier. Shannon, in addition to being the office manager, ran the volunteer program, so Annabeth frequently saw her at the intake desk interacting with volunteers.

"Morning," Annabeth greeted her.

"Good morning. How are you doing?"

"Good," Annabeth said.

"Zoey and I went to your office yesterday afternoon to check on you, but you'd already left."

"I'm okay," Annabeth assured her. Annabeth considered saying she had an appointment, which was why she wasn't in her office when they stopped in. But that was overcompensating, she thought. Plus, it might lead to the question of how she could've gone to an appointment with her car still in the lot this morning, which would lead to Cooper's dead battery explanation. Oh, that whole fib might quickly spin out of control. Besides, she really didn't want to talk about what had happened.

"Do you have any idea what the guy wanted? I mean, why come to a rescue?"

"I guess that's the sixty-four-thousand-dollar question," Annabeth said. "No idea. It all happened so fast. I'm just glad Cooper wasn't hurt after struggling with the guy."

"Me too. Do the police have any leads?"

"I don't know. I haven't spoken to them since it happened. I'll probably talk to a detective today," she said.

"A detective? Wow. If I can do anything, just let me know."

"They are taking it seriously. Thank you. That's very kind."

"It's so weird. And it's really horrible with you being so new. I hope you won't hold it against us."

It was meant to be witty, so Annabeth obliged and smiled. "I don't." Shannon was concerned; Annabeth could see it in her face. She did appreciate it. Annabeth turned to Stanley. "Do you know what happened to the puppy that came in yesterday? Did she get placed with a foster?"

Stanley punched a few keys on the keyboard. He shook his head. "No, it doesn't look like it," he said, continuing to punch keys.

"No, she wasn't placed?"

"No, I'm not showing any puppies from yesterday."

"That's odd. She was definitely here. Can you try the name Solstice?"

He punched more keys. "The last Solstice was three years ago."

"Maybe she was logged in some other way? I saw her in the kennel yesterday as an overnight drop off. Black Labrador puppy."

"No new arrivals yesterday. Dogs or cats."

"That doesn't make sense. I saw the dog. Both in the overnight drop-off kennel and later in the warehouse. I named her. She had paperwork. On a clip board. Solstice written at the top."

"I don't know," the volunteer said, a little like a wild animal in headlights.

"Ruthie made calls yesterday to try to find a foster for her," Annabeth added as if to further prove the dog had been there.

"It's possible the owner was found," Shannon offered.

Annabeth didn't know all the nuances of the program yet, but that didn't sound right. If an owner had come looking for the dog, Paws charged a kind of "finder's fee." Annabeth had enough to worry about. She told herself she should just drop it. But she couldn't. "Wouldn't there still be a record? Even if an owner showed up?" She looked between Stanley and Shannon.

Shannon bobbed her head in a way that it was unclear if she were nodding yes or shaking no. "Yes," she finally admitted. "But sometimes, if the dog hasn't been put in the system and hasn't cost us anything—meaning a vet hasn't spent time with it yet and there's no meds or whatever—we just hand the dog over and tell them to get the dog chipped in case it gets lost again."

The finder's fee was minimal, $25. But Annabeth couldn't help but wonder how often it happened. She started doing the math in her head to calculate what that could mean for lost income to the rescue.

As if reading her mind, Shannon said, "It doesn't happen often. Once in a great while. But it does happen. Well, I better get back to work. Stanley, let me know when you need to leave so I can cover the desk until the afternoon volunteer arrives. Annabeth, I really mean it, if you need anything or I can help you, let me know."

Annabeth smiled. "I appreciate it."

"Dentist appointment," Stanley said pointing to his jaw.

Annabeth plopped down in the chair behind her desk. It was a good thing that Solstice (or whatever her name was) was reunited with her family. So, why did it upset her? Somewhere in the back of her mind, had she already decided to adopt the dog?

While pondering the question, Annabeth noticed one of her file cabinet drawers open. Just a fraction of an inch. But, still, it was open. In her haste to get to Whittier yesterday, had she forgotten to lock it?

None of the files inside seemed amiss, but when she shut the drawer, she noticed tiny scratches on the lock. Had those always been there?

Then she looked around her entire office. It wasn't anything obvious. But now she noticed both stacks of files on her desk were askew rather than in the neat uniform way she kept them. And what about the bottom drawer of her desk? It, too, was opened a few inches.

The more she looked around, the more certain she became that someone had riffled through her office. It was subtle, nothing big, but several little things just weren't right. A few more minutes examining everything from the center of the room and she became absolutely certain that it was not as she had left it the night before.

~ * ~

"What am I not going to believe? Tell me," Cooper implored when she burst through his door telling him he wasn't going to believe what she'd just discovered.

"Come," she said, motioning with her hand for him to follow. Cooper followed her back to her office. She stopped in the middle of the room again.

"What?" he asked.

"Someone's been in here." Cooper looked around and she could read it from his eyes and the look on his face that he didn't see it.

"Are you sure?"

"I'm sure," she said. Then she spent the next few minutes showing him the office through her eyes. Cooper had only been back for a couple days. He didn't know her work style. She explained how she was meticulous when it came to her files and paperwork, how she checked and double checked that cabinets were locked.

At the end, Cooper asked, "Are you okay?"

"Yes," she said, and surprised herself by actually feeling okay. Compared to everything else, this didn't seem that scary. How weird was that? Someone could break into her office, riffle through her things and, compared to the previous two days, it seemed relatively innocuous. That was seriously screwed up.

And then Cooper said, "What the hell is this guy looking for?" She knew it wasn't a question she need answer. "It had to have been after closing time yesterday, or someone would've noticed a person wandering back here to the offices, especially after my email yesterday."

"Someone isn't always at the intake desk," Annabeth said, thinking of Stanley leaving early. "But there's no way a person could be wandering around without someone noticing."

"Agreed. It's not possible," Cooper said. He walked to the file cabinet and looked closely at the scratches around the lock.

"Shannon said she and Zoey came to my office yesterday after we'd left but, just like you, they wouldn't have noticed anything because it's not obvious."

"But we just agreed it had to have happened after hours."

"I know. I'm just saying. You're right, irrelevant. Maybe I am a little flustered. Confused. Angry. I don't know."

In the end, what was there to do? Annabeth called Officer Weir, the policewoman who'd taken her statement on Tuesday night, since Annabeth still hadn't received a call from the detective assigned to the case. She got voice mail, presumably because the officer worked in the evening. Annabeth left a message explaining the latest incident.

Neither of them felt very confident the police would be able to do anything. It was Cooper's idea to photograph everything. At least it would serve as a record. It might not look like much to someone viewing the images, but Annabeth could explain. Someone going through her office and taking nothing didn't rise to the same level as being held at gunpoint. Even being held at gunpoint was beginning to look like it didn't warrant a followup call from the detective.

"I'm more and more convinced, the best thing we can do," Cooper said after they finished with the photos, "is to figure out what this is all about."

He was right. Long shot or not, it was time for her to start looking at the vendors and invoices. What else could she do? Leaving for the day wouldn't help. She'd never be able to stop running things through her mind. And, if she left, where would she go? Daytime at work seemed like the safest place.

Like the day before, Annabeth worked until her eyes hurt and her body was stiff. She only stopped when Zoey poked her head in to say she was ordering Chinese food for lunch and did Annabeth want anything. She did. When the food arrived, Annabeth ate with the others who ordered, including Cooper, in their small conference room.

There was a lot of talk about Cooper's bruised face and rehashing what had happened. The more people talked, the more unsettled they seemed. But Annabeth knew that talking it through was how they were processing what had happened in their work place. It was upsetting. Besides, wasn't that the same thing she and Cooper were doing?

Cooper sat across from her, and several times he caught her looking at him. Such a genuinely good guy, she thought again, and had to stop herself from thinking about his wavy hair and wondering if he had those same butterscotch curls on his chest since, it had turned out, he did have an extra t-shirt in that duffel bag.

At 4:00 Cooper came to her office to see how she was progressing.

"Nada," Annabeth said. "I checked all invoices over a thousand dollars for the last five years. I verified that every vendor for the last ten years has a business license with the State of Alaska. Now, a smart thief would get a business license because they are so easy to check. But the businesses also list the owners' names and there was nothing fishy I could see."

"You ready to call this lead a dead end?" he asked without judgment.

"Yes. In fact, what I'm more inclined to admit is that it was no lead at all. It was just a random out-there theory. But whatever we want to call it—yes—it is officially dead."

"Speaking of out-there thoughts, I've been wondering if it was about robbery. I know we've been over this, but is there any chance he just didn't see your purse? He would've been operating on adrenaline."

"Then what did he want me to tell him? Where was he taking me? And, if it were true, why come back when I'm not even in the office? No, I feel sure it wasn't about stealing from me."

"You're right. It was just a random thought I'd had. So, I was thinking I'd follow you home tonight so your car doesn't have to stay in the parking lot another night. I know it's early, but I was thinking of leaving in a few minutes."

Annabeth noticed he didn't say what would come next, after he followed her home. "Sure," she said.

"I'm running on fumes. Not me, but my truck. I should've stopped for gas on the way here this morning."

"Go ahead. I'll finish up here and meet you at my apartment then? I assume you remember how to get there?"

"Okay," he said. "But don't go inside. I'd rather you wait for me so I can look around first."

Outside her apartment building, Annabeth pulled into a parking space with an empty spot on either side so Cooper could park next to her. She put the car in park but didn't turn it off. It was too cold for that.

Her mind went back to the puppy. She wondered how the little girl, little Solstice, was doing and hoped she had a good and kind family.

Even if Annabeth wouldn't be adopting that particular pup, she could start thinking about a different one. There were plenty in need of a home.

Cooper's truck pulled into the spot on the passenger's side. From the lights in the parking lot, she could see into his truck. He smiled when he caught her looking at him.

Annabeth got out of her car and went to his truck.

"I hope you weren't waiting long."

"Nope."

"Here," he said and handed her a grocery bag. "I stopped at the store."

She'd been so lost in thought about the dog and about a house with a yard where a dog could run that she hadn't realized quite how long she'd been sitting there. She couldn't believe he'd both filled up his gas tank and gone to the grocery store.

"I'll get the rest," he said.

Exactly how much grocery shopping had he done? Annabeth started toward her building.

"Hey," he called from his truck. "Let me go inside first."

Yeah, yeah, she thought. She waved to him as she saw him thread the handle of a third plastic grocery bag over his arm.

At the door of her ground floor apartment, she inserted her key in the lock. She'd wait but at least she could have the door open.

Annabeth swung open the door. And froze.

She couldn't move. Couldn't breathe.

Once again, she was face-to-face with her assailant.

Thirteen

Cooper caught something out of the corner of his eye. He turned to look and saw Annabeth running.

"It's him," she shouted, waving her arm and pointing a finger toward the blur that buzzed by in his peripheral vision.

He didn't see the man's face because, by the time Cooper looked in the direction Annabeth pointed, he only saw the backside of a running figure. It didn't matter. Cooper knew. Instinct. Tallness. Annabeth's reaction. He knew.

Cooper dropped the grocery bags and took off after him. He crossed the parking lot quickly. Once outside the range of the parking lot lights, he had to slow. But so did the tall man. It was hard to be surefooted as they headed down the sidewalk toward the hiking and biking trails. Orange glow cast by city lights provided some illumination, but the sidewalks were not clear, interspersed with drifts of snow and ice patches. Cooper wanted to sprint after him, but he just couldn't. At least they were both fighting the same obstacles.

The tall man had the advantage of long legs. But his long strides were no match for Cooper's fitness level. Even though he hadn't been to the gym in more than two months, he thought he'd be able to catch the man. Within a block, Cooper decreased the guy's lead by half.

Another block, and he should be able to overtake him with half a block to spare before the man made it to the wooded area.

If he got that far, the odds of catching him decreased dramatically. With so many twists and turns and trees for cover, he could easily hide, making it almost impossible for Cooper to find him. Like his previous encounter with the lanky man, Cooper had nothing. No flashlight. No weapon. But that didn't matter.

The idea of catching this guy, ensuring Annabeth was truly out of harm's way, pushed him even harder. This whole ordeal was almost over. He just needed to catch the guy.

The blast so startled Cooper he fell backward to the ground as if he'd actually been hit.

The man, still running, had pulled out a gun and shot in Cooper's direction. He didn't aim, only fired in the direction behind him to slow Cooper. It worked.

Cooper jumped to his feet again. But he'd lost momentum and distance. Now, it was only with luck he'd reach the man before he disappeared into the trees. Cooper cleared everything from his mind but the figure in front of him. He needed to do this for Annabeth.

He pushed hard to close the distance between them once again.

Half a block from the wooded area, he was surprised when the tall man stopped and turned to face him. In another hand-to-hand battle, Cooper felt confident he could take him. But the man had no intention of that.

Cooper saw the man raise the gun. Unlike the first shot, this time he was taking aim. Cooper had no choice but to dive over and behind a snow berm just seconds before the shot cut through the cold night.

A second shot cracked the air and Cooper heard it hit not more than a few feet from where he lay. It hit a tree and bark splintered off, several pieces reaching him.

A third shot landed even closer, barreling through the soft snow behind him, causing a white explosion. Cooper ducked. A berm wasn't exactly good cover, but there was no place safer nearby. He stayed out of the line of sight of the tall man and his gun.

Seconds passed without a sound. When Cooper dared looked up, the man had disappeared into the woods.

He cursed aloud and punched at the snow, the chance to cement Annabeth's safety gone.

He sat where he landed until he caught his breath and his heart slowed. Just as he was about to stand, Annabeth dropped by his side.

"Oh my God," she cried. "Are you shot? I heard shots." She patted him down, looking for his wound, her breathing even more ragged than his.

Cooper clasped her hands in his. "I'm okay. I am. The guy's a terrible shot, only trying to scare me, to slow me down." He wasn't entirely sure if that were true, but he didn't want to cause more panic.

"I heard shots," she said again, her voice cracking.

"I'm fine. I'm fine," he tried to reassure her. "I'm no dummy. When the bullets started flying, I took a dive."

She laughed. "I'm glad." She wrapped her arms around his neck and held on tight. Cooper found himself thinking it was almost worth nearly getting shot at.

When she released him, her face stayed just inches from his. "I'd never forgive myself if something happened to you," she said. If Cooper didn't know better, he'd have thought she was going to kiss him.

But she'd made her feelings quite clear the night before.

"Nothing will happen to me. I promise," he said. "Now help me up."

Annabeth rose slowly and helped him to his feet. When she told him to lean on her as they walked back to her apartment, he did as she instructed. There might not be kissing, but he wasn't going to turn down the chance to be close to her, even if he didn't need the assistance walking.

After gathering the spilled groceries both at his truck and outside her apartment door, they went inside.

Annabeth surprised and impressed him by remaining calm as she surveyed her apartment. It was a mess. Books pulled from the two bookcases, drawers opened and the contents strewn, clothes flung from their hangers, two potted plants on their sides.

"This goes without saying," Cooper said, "but I'm saying it anyway, you aren't staying here tonight. Get your things. I'm getting you out of here."

Annabeth didn't protest. She turned and went to her bedroom to pack a bag.

He surveyed the room again. Raising four boys, his mother often described the state of their rooms as the Tasmanian Devil sprinting through during a hurricane. That's what her apartment made him think of now.

He bent down to right a plant and instantly pulled his hand away. He stood and called toward the room, "Wait. Don't touch anything."

"What?" she said, standing in the doorway to her bedroom, a shirt in hand. "What's the matter?"

"We need to call the police," he said, trying to keep his voice even, to convey calmness.

She looked blankly at him. Then blinked and shook her head as if to clear her mind. "It didn't even occur to me. I just want to get out of here before he comes back again. Not to mention, we've already called them once today."

"I know," Cooper said. If he hadn't been so focused on getting her out of harm's way, he might have thought to call them immediately. "The guy had on gloves, just like the night at Paws, so I doubt there are fingerprints to be found, but you never know."

"I didn't notice the gloves," she said. "Then again, I didn't on Tuesday either."

"At the very least, they will want to take photos so don't disturb anything."

"Yeah," she agreed, but made no move toward her phone. She looked around the room as if seeing it for the first time. "Look, I know we need to call the cops but I just don't know if I have it in me. Can't we leave everything untouched and—I don't know—go wherever we were going to go?"

He knew the correct answer was to say they absolutely could not. The police needed to be called. Cooper looked at Annabeth and his resolve melted. Leaving was a terrible idea. Then again, he decided to verbalize what he'd been thinking just before he reached for the plant. "Is it just me or does it seem like he wasn't really looking for anything?"

Annabeth shifted the shirt from one hand to the other and waved it into the bedroom. "You know, it's funny you say that because I was thinking the exact same in here. My clothes are everywhere but, yeah, it doesn't look like a search as much as just a mess. Today at the office my things were off, like someone didn't know how precise I like things, but was definitely trying to be careful. I don't think we were supposed to notice the office search. But this—" Annabeth spread her arms like she was presenting the room for display.

"Agreed. It may not feel like it, but I don't think he was waiting for you, either. We left the office earlier than we would've if we hadn't noticed your office. What time do you normally get home? About six-thirty?"

"Yes, six-twenty, six-thirty. But today I opened the front door before five-thirty, before Paws is even closed for the day," Annabeth added.

"I think he did this to—"

They both finished the sentence at the same time. "—to scare you," Cooper said while Annabeth said, "—to scare me."

"This doesn't really scare me. That's not true. It scares me. He scares me. But this? It's more like I'm mad. I'm mad at this mess, and that he got into my apartment. Maybe I'll feel afraid after it has sunk in."

"Probably."

"And anyway, what is he scaring me from?"

Cooper shook his head. No clue.

"Just like at Paws, it's like he walked in through the wall. No sign of a break-in. He was just in. He isn't going to stop until he finds what he's looking for."

"If he wasn't here to do a real search, maybe he was trying to scare you from going back into the office. That's where this started."

"Maybe." She sounded a little vacant, distant. It was possible she was in a bit of shock or talking about it was making the fear sink in. This was probably bringing up Tuesday night all over again. "Maybe," she said again.

"I almost had myself convinced that first night was random. That he was looking for money and just missed seeing your purse. But after this, no way. Once again, we are back to the same question we keep asking, what was he looking for at Paws? Why doesn't he want you in the office?"

Annabeth interrupted him. "And why now?" she added.

"Why now?" he repeated. "It still might be about you, the accountant, but after today, it's crossed over because now it's also about you the person. I will not permit that."

"What are you saying?" she asked.

Against his better judgment he said, "I'm saying pack enough for a few days and we'll call Weir once we get to where we are going."

She didn't argue and returned to the bedroom.

Fourteen

Annabeth hadn't noticed the gloves. Could've been the winter weather as easily as it could've been not to leave prints. She wasn't inclined to think the tall man was particularly bright, but anyone who ever watched television would know to wear gloves if you were going to commit a crime.

Her bedroom, like the living room, would take a couple hours to put back in order. Clothes needed hanging, more needed to be folded and returned to their place in drawers. Shoes needed to find their mates and be returned to their proper place in the closet. But that would have wait.

At the very least, though, she needed to clear a path. They certainly wouldn't print every item of clothes. Could they even lift prints from fabric? She gathered armloads of clothes from the floor and tossed them on the bed. She might as well make use of the bed space since she wouldn't be sleeping in her own bed tonight. Maybe longer.

As she sorted through the clothes looking for what to bring, she watched the scene like a movie reel in her mind. She had opened her apartment door and seen the man. He stood with a shocked look on his face, eyes wide. Like he was surprised to see her. A second later, he gained his composure and barreled toward her. Annabeth had braced herself for the worst. She could still feel how her body went rigid in anticipation of a tackle like the one Cooper had received. But instead of plowing her down, he shoved her hard out of his path. She dropped the bag of groceries as she slammed against the wall. But he continued on past. Once she got her footing, she started yelling and running after him.

For all he knew, Annabeth was alone. Yet he didn't come after her. Didn't speak to her. He only wanted to get away, which begged the questions: Why didn't he come after her? Why didn't he ask again about the money or whatever he wanted? It's possible the surprise of seeing her caused him to panic.

She asked herself what was going on even as she ran after him, yelling to Cooper. She followed both men in the chase as Cooper gained on the guy and then both were out of sight.

Sheer terror. It's the only way to describe what came to mind as Annabeth recalled hearing shots ring out. The movie reel black. She was too far behind to see what was happening because she wasn't nimble over the snow and ice. She pressed on, willing herself to get to Cooper.

They should have just let the guy go.

When she saw Cooper's head rising above the snow, it was obvious he was down. Her entire insides turned to jelly. She was so sure he'd been hit. Even now, that sinking feeling lingered throughout her insides.

The doors of the closet stood wide open, making it easy to find a small suitcase pushed to one side without having to touch anything.

The relief she had felt to find him alive, not injured at all, was so overwhelming she wanted to cry. Her heart ached—then and now—at the idea of what might have happened. She never would've forgiven herself if she had got him shot.

Annabeth folded a few outfits from the bed into the suitcase. Then added undergarments and her favorite winter pajamas—gray flannel covered in tiny yellow stars and white moons.

The man didn't do anything in the bathroom. Annabeth was grateful for that because cosmetics and other products strewn around would've made a real mess. Though sure he hadn't been in there, she still took care to not touch more than she had to. She caught a glimpse of herself in the mirror. Disheveled, to be sure. Tired. Defeated.

She tried to tidy her hair as the movie continued to roll, sitting in the snow with Cooper. Despite all good sense, she had nearly kissed him. In the mirror, she caught herself blushing. Just a little. When she released him from the hug, they were still so close. Just inches from each other's face, each other's lips. She didn't care about what she'd said the night before in the B&B. Everything in her mind and her body screamed out to kiss him.

Just as she leaned ever-so-slightly forward to meet his lips, he asked her to help him stand. And the spell was broken. The moment gone. Her own good sense flooded back to her brain and body.

Annabeth added toiletries to the suitcase. She looked around the room. Even though she felt more anger than fear, she could admit to herself that she was glad Cooper insisted she wouldn't be staying here tonight. She shut the suitcase and joined Cooper in the living room. It did make her wonder though, where was he taking her?

~ * ~

When they hit the outskirts of town, Annabeth found Officer Weir's card. Like earlier in the day, she went to voicemail. She left another message. It was brief, but she conveyed the break-in, the mess, and that she was staying somewhere other than her apartment for a night or two. She decided to wait for the callback to explain they hadn't touched anything and to buy time to think up a good reason why they hadn't called 911 and waited for the police. Annabeth knew there was no good reason. Or not a good enough one, anyway. But she'd cross that hurdle when it arose. Then she leaned back in the seat of Cooper's pickup and stared out the window into the dark night.

They'd been on the road heading north—opposite of their south trip route to Whittier 24 hours earlier—for nearly an hour before Annabeth began to wonder where they were going. She'd assumed he was taking her to his house, remembering the offer of his extra bedroom. Was that just yesterday when he had made the offer or that first night? It blended together now.

She'd assumed he lived in town but, in hindsight, realized he never actually said that. "Do you drive this every day?" she asked, not envying such a tedious commute, especially in the dark snowy winter months.

"What?" he said, turning down the radio. "Sorry, I didn't hear you. I'm in my own world, still trying to work things out. Wondering if we are missing something obvious."

"I know. I've been doing the same. I asked if this was your daily commute. It's such a long way to drive."

"No," he said. "I live in town."

"Where are we going then? You aren't teaching me about camping tonight, are you?"

Cooper laughed. "Can't tonight. We ate all the good backpacker meals last night. Plus, the tent is at home. No, there's a cabin out here. I don't know, I just wanted to be extra cautious, and I figure if that guy can find out where you live, it probably wouldn't be hard for him to figure out where I live, too. Just in case we're wrong about why he was at your place, I don't want him trying to get to you at mine."

"I didn't know you had a cabin," she said.

"There's lots of things you don't know about me. It won't be too much longer. Another ten miles to the turnoff."

"Like what? Tell me one more thing I don't know about you," Annabeth said, glad for the reprieve from her own thoughts.

"'Hmm, let's see. One thing? I feel like you got an earful when we were locked in the tunnel. But if I have to say—"

"You do," she laughed.

"Okay, how's this? My favorite color is red. I skipped the third grade. I'm allergic to shellfish. And, let's see, I hope this doesn't detract from my manliness, but I really don't like the taste of beer. There. That's four things."

"Those are good things," she said. She wanted to add that she doubted there was anything he could do to detract (or distract) her thoughts about his masculinity, but decided that was a thought best kept to herself.

"Now you tell me one," Cooper said.

"Okay." She thought a moment. "This is a really new one and, before yesterday I probably wasn't going to do it but, I've been thinking about it and I've decided. I am going to adopt a dog."

"Ahh, Annabeth, that's fantastic. You will love it. I promise. Once you've had a dog in your life, you'll wonder how you ever got along without one. More importantly, you'll wonder why you'd ever want to. It's funny you should say that because I've been thinking that, after the holidays, I might be ready for another one, too."

"Our dogs can be buddies."

"Good idea. You said you'd been considering it since you started working at Paws, so I know it isn't just a reaction to the last few days. You wouldn't want to adopt one for the wrong reason. Like fear. True, dogs are a kind of security system since they bark if they hear something. Which, at the same time, is something that will drive you crazy. But a dog cannot keep you entirely safe."

Cooper slowed and then turned onto a road off the highway, driving much slower in the snow ruts along a road that didn't look often plowed.

"I know. I just realized something," Annabeth said.

"Tell me."

"You flew back into town on Monday, went to work on Tuesday when all this insanity started."

"Yes," he agreed.

"Except for Monday, you haven't even really been home. Now, for a third night in a row, you haven't slept in your own bed. I hate that. It makes me feel even worse than I did before. And especially after all you've been through. Not to mention two of those nights you were on a couch."

"It's fine. I'll be in a bed tonight," he said, a hint of seduction in his voice. Annabeth wondered what he meant by that. "Actually, and I'm not saying I'm glad any of this is happening, but it has kept my mind off losing my mother."

"And your wife and your dog," Annabeth added.

"Pretty much off the last year of my life."

"I mean, I guess I shouldn't have presumed. Wait, did you say you'll be in your own bed tonight? You said no one will find *me* here."

Cooper turned onto a single lane road that, as near as Annabeth could tell, was dirt underneath the snow pack. They must be really close.

Annabeth wanted to tell him she was glad he wasn't as sad anymore, but she couldn't find the right words. She also wanted to express how she hoped he wasn't just dropping her off there. Alone, in the woods. She liked his company, his presence. He did make her feel safer. She liked him. "Are you leaving me out here?"

Cooper pulled up to a cabin and stopped. The little cabin confused her. She looked to Cooper then back at the cabin. Smoke curled from the chimney and a glow from lights inside filled the window. Someone was already inside. Then she remembered he never said he was taking her to *his* cabin, he said he was taking her to a cabin.

"Are you kidding? Of course, I'm not leaving you alone." Cooper pointed to the cabin and said, "My brother's here. This is his cabin."

Fifteen

As expected, Rusty came out the cabin's door and stood on the small porch, a shotgun and his German Shepherd, Moose, by his side.

Cooper flashed his headlights at his brother, then turned them and the truck off.

Rusty waved and went back inside. Moose followed.

Annabeth opened the door and hopped down from the seat in the truck.

Cooper saw her reach in the truck's bed for her suitcase and said, "Leave that here for now. Let's go inside and I'll introduce you."

The cabin was small and simple but cozy. It included a bedroom, then an open floor plan with a sitting area, kitchen and small dining area. A black, big-bellied wood stove stood in the middle, heating the entire place. Rusty sat in the handmade wooden rocking chair, while Moose curled up on his dog bed by the stove.

"You could've got your head blown off," Rusty said, skipping the hellos and howdy-dos. "Why didn't you call first?"

"Check your phone, genius," Cooper said. "I called an hour ago to say I was coming out and bringing someone."

Rusty turned his eyes to Annabeth as if just at that moment he noticed a third person in the room.

"Hi," she said. "Annabeth Neilson."

Rusty nodded his hello. He turned back to his brother. "You expect me to believe you got a new girlfriend since I saw you Monday? And what the hell happened to your face?"

Cooper smiled. His brother could be a bit caustic, and maybe he had reason to be, but he was a good person with a big heart. Cooper had been overlooking Rusty's hard edge for years, so generally wasn't ruffled by anything big bro said or did. He turned to Annabeth to explain. "We came back from Florida on the same flight." Then he turned to his brother. "She's not my girlfriend, she's a co-worker. And she's in trouble."

Rusty continued to look between the two. "Okay, then," he finally said.

"Now, I'm going to bring in a few groceries while you offer Annabeth a drink. Then I'll tell you everything over dinner," Cooper said.

"Okay, then," Rusty repeated.

Outside, Cooper had to smile in the dark night. His brother. 'Such a character' was how he was most often described. He'd pretty much come out from the womb as a grumpy old man. He matched his name like no other man Cooper knew. The caustic part came after six years in the military and three tours in Iraq.

Cooper rearranged items among the grocery sacks until everything he needed was in one. He returned to the cabin where he found Annabeth sitting at the kitchen table with a glass of red wine in front of her. He put the bag on the counter and started unloading it as he watched Rusty dump saltine crackers into a bowl and set them on the table in front of Annabeth, Rusty's attempt at hospitality by offering an appetizer. Cooper rolled his eyes, though he didn't say a word.

"How about frittatas?" Cooper asked as he rolled up his sleeves to wash his hands. Luckily, the bag with the eggs had been the last one still sitting in his truck when he had dropped the others to give chase.

Cooper worked in the kitchen with the assistance of Rusty. Annabeth offered to help, but they said no. They had dinner covered. It was a recipe—one of several—their mother had taught all her sons to make. Without needing to ask, Rusty pulled out a package of moose sausage from the freezer. Normally, they would slice the sausage and include it in the dish. But since Annabeth was vegetarian, Cooper kept the sausage in links and cooked them in a separate pan.

Now and again, Cooper would look over at Annabeth, and each time he was rewarded with a smile. The sweetest smile. The brightest eyes. Rusty even refilled her wine glass without prompting. She had that kind of effect, he thought.

Once the frittata, thick with sliced mushrooms, diced onions, orange bell peppers and shredded zucchini, was finished, Cooper put a lid on it while the sausages finished. Then dinner was served. Cooper divided the frittata into thirds and plated his creation. He added two sausage links to his and his brother's plates.

"Smells wonderful," Annabeth said as he set it in front of her.

After adding salt, pepper, hot sauce, silverware and napkins to the table, they were ready to dig in.

As soon as Cooper was seated, Rusty, who'd already stabbed a sausage link with his fork and had it half eaten, said, "Start talking."

Cooper shared the *Reader's Digest* version of the events since the brothers had said goodbye at the airport Monday night. He skipped the theories and the part about getting locked in the tunnel between the BTI building and the school. He also left out the part where he and Annabeth ended up in the same room at Mrs. B's B&B in Whittier. No reason to cloud the issue. Or, really, to give his brother fodder for embarrassing him or otherwise teasing him relentlessly for the foreseeable future.

Rusty listened intently, once putting his finger in the air for Cooper to pause the story while Rusty got up to add more links to his plate.

"That brings us to the present," Cooper told his brother when he returned to his seat. "I thought it best to keep Annabeth away from where this monster could find her."

"Good idea," Rusty said. "So the police couldn't offer any protection after you were shot at? What did they say?"

Cooper knew it wasn't his brightest moment when he had agreed with Annabeth they didn't need to call 911. But hearing Rusty ask the question, he now understood what a poor decision it was. He turned to Annabeth to see her reaction.

"We didn't call the police," she said, offering him an out. "Well, we did. Just not how you might think."

"Exactly how many ways are there to call the police?" Rusty looked back and forth between the two.

"We left a message for the officer who took our statement on Tuesday," Annabeth explained.

"What?" Rusty said, half surprised and half irritated, turning to Cooper for a better explanation.

"I was so focused on getting Annabeth out of there. We called and left a message when we realized her office had been sifted through, but—"

"He was in her house," Rusty said emphatically. "Not to mention someone shot at you, brother," Rusty said and hit his fist on the table which stirred Moose to look up from his place next to the wood stove. "You don't mess around when people are shooting at you. I should know."

Annabeth reached out and touched Rusty on the arm. "We will make sure to talk to someone tomorrow. Promise."

"Okay," he said and unclenched his fist. "For all you know, someone probably already did. If the neighbors heard gunshots, the police might already know, but they have no way to connect it to what happened to you two at Paws."

"I promise," Annabeth said. "You're absolutely right. With everything else we didn't think it through. If I don't hear back from a detective by tomorrow morning, I'll call again."

"You should call tonight," Rusty said to Cooper.

"It's late, and we're tired. Annabeth promised. She doesn't lie," Cooper said, though, of course, he had no way to know if that were actually true. And promising didn't lessen his guilt at having made the wrong decision.

"Unlike you," his brother predictably tacked on.

"She's safe here and that's the important thing," Cooper said.

"At least take one of Dad's guns," Rusty said.

"No."

"A small handgun. Come on. For protection," Rusty said. "I'll even give you a refresher. Without any snide remarks or attitude."

"Why don't I do these dishes while you two work it out?" Annabeth said and stood.

"Sit," Cooper said. "We're going to get going. This guy can handle a few dishes."

Rusty took his own plate as well as his brother's and set them on the floor. "Moose," he called. Moose was across the room in a couple strides as if he knew one of the plates was going to net him half a fat, juicy sausage. He swallowed it whole. "The pre-wash cycle," Rusty said.

A confused looked crossed Annabeth's brows. "We're going?" she asked Cooper. "I thought—" she spread her arm out to the cabin.

"What? You thought I was going to leave you here with his one? No way. I wouldn't subject you to that kind of misery," Cooper said, slapping his brother on the shoulder. Then Cooper turned serious and said, "You'll keep an eye out, right?"

"No," his brother said back, equally as serious. But Cooper knew that was his Rusty-way of saying yes, and I love you, bro.

Cooper stood and Annabeth followed.

At the door, Rusty asked if he were sure about the gun. But Cooper declined. Guns, hunting, fishing. Those were Rusty's things, and their dad's when he'd been alive. Not Cooper's. Cooper enjoyed the outdoors as much as they did, but in a different way. Give him a backpack and a mountain to climb any day over tracking prey or casting a fishing line.

Moose sprinted out when Rusty opened the door and disappeared into the woods. "Nightly business," Rusty said, as though someone had asked where the dog was going.

Annabeth hugged Rusty, thanked him. Cooper could visibly see his brother's hard exterior softening. Yeah, Cooper knew, his brother was all bark on the outside but just a gooey filling inside. Cooper also hugged his brother goodbye and told him they'd keep him in the loop.

Inside the truck, Annabeth asked, "So, if I'm not staying here, where are you taking me?"

"It's a surprise," Cooper said mischievously.

He started the truck and followed the road around behind Rusty's cabin and down a little way. She hadn't even had time to get settled and buckle her seat belt before he turned off the truck's engine.

"My cabin," Cooper said, pointing to the structure that looked nearly identical to the one they had just left. The only difference was this one lacked the billowy smoke from the chimney and the warm glow of someone inside.

He saw Annabeth smiling in the dark.

She carried the four remaining grocery bags inside while he got her suitcase and his duffel bag.

"Keep your coat on," he said inside. "It's going to be cold. We aren't so remote that we are off grid, but the stove takes a while to heat the place." He flipped a switch and a floor lamp came on.

"It looks the same from the outside, but—" she said.

"Technically, I share this cabin with our youngest brother, Brody, but he never comes out here. If I would've known he'd never come out, I would've built this one like Rusty's. Instead, I made two tiny bedrooms instead of his one big one." Cooper opened the damper on the wood stove and started stuffing wood into the belly.

"You built this? I'm impressed," Annabeth said, walking around the room.

"Don't be. We had a lot of help. It only means I know how to pound nails with a hammer." He balled up sheets of newspaper and stuffed several wads under the wood, added a fire starter stick, then took a lighter and started fire in several places.

"Is this you and your brothers?" Annabeth asked. He looked up to see her standing in front of a framed photo of him and his brothers as kids on a shelf alongside a few books and a bowl of rocks he'd picked up on various hikes over the years. He watched as she took it down. "The little one is Brody. That's easy."

"William is the oldest. Named after our dad. Then it's Rusty and me."

"Which one is you and which is Rusty? You look the same size." She looked up at him. "Are you two twins?"

"He wishes," Cooper laughed. "We're a year apart. To the day. We hated sharing the same birthday when we were kids. I'm the one on the left."

He watched her study the photo. She caught him staring at her when she looked up. "But you're the only one called Cooper?"

"That's Rusty's fault, too. Let's just say he's the source of most of my problems," Cooper laughed. "He couldn't say Malcolm and somehow, over time, Malcolm Cooper turned into just Cooper because he could say that. And everyone started calling me that and Malcolm never really took."

Annabeth returned the photo to its place on the shelf.

Once Cooper was sure one of the logs had caught fire, he closed the door to the stove. "Come on. I want to show you something."

He took Annabeth's hand and led her outside. It was cold but, in truth, it didn't seem much colder than the inside of the cabin. The snow was up to their knees as he plowed through, telling her to follow in his footsteps to try to keep snow out of her shoes.

It wasn't more than five or six minutes before the trees thinned as they crested a small hill. Then they stood in a clearing.

The black sky rounded down over them like the dome of an observatory. Once outside the city, a person could actually see the true color of night. The clouds that cast the orange glow from the bouncing city lights in Anchorage had moved on to make for a cloudless sky, clear and blanketed in stars.

As beautiful as both were, it wasn't the reason he had brought her out there. Off to the east, a curtain of color danced in the sky. A giant sheet, a slow-moving wave of light. The aurora borealis. The Northern Lights.

He moved aside so Annabeth could stand in front of him.

"Oh!" Annabeth caught her breath.

They both stood and stared in awe. It was stunning. While most Northern Lights were green, tonight they were spectators to a particularly beautiful show of red, green, blue, purple, and yellow.

"I don't think I've ever seen so many of the colors," she said. "You can't see much in town."

"I know. Rusty told me they were out tonight when we were leaving. He thought you'd like to see them."

"Yes," she whispered. "Yes."

Annabeth surprised him when she leaned back into his chest. Without thought, he wrapped his arms around her shoulders and she sunk further into him. He wrapped his arms tighter, looked up at the glorious sky and basked in the glow of the moment.

Sixteen

The big, black moonless sky. The slow-moving gossamer curtain of color. The cold. The feeling like they were the only two people standing on earth at that moment. Magical. It was the only word Annabeth could come up with to describe it. Describing her feelings was a more complex task.

The battle that raged in her mind was the same as the night before. Cooper had so plainly told her he didn't want to be alone and getting involved with him when he wasn't yet finished grieving the loss of his wife would make her his transition person. And, by their nature, a transitional relationship would be short-lived. And where would that leave her? As the woman who had an affair with her boss. Yet again. And having to leave another job.

As much as she felt the desire to be close to him, she needed to stay steadfast in her resolve to be a better version of herself than she had been in the past. Starting the new job at Paws wasn't just about a new job. It was about creating a new life with a new narrative about the kind of person she was.

She involuntarily did a full body shiver. The dark night, despite the magic of the moment, still seeped cold into her bones. Her ankles were blocks of ice from the snow that had gotten under her pant legs and in her shoes as they walked in the deep snow. Annabeth stepped out of his embrace and turned to face him. "Thank you for showing me this. It's lovely. But I'm freezing, so can we go back?"

"Sure," he said. They turned and followed the path they'd cut back to Cooper's cabin. Before entering, they stomped around the porch, shaking the stuck-on snow off their legs. Inside, they removed their coats and shoes, but the cabin was still quite chilly.

It would take a little time for the burning wood to turn to the hot coals needed for real warmth. Annabeth opened her small suitcase and found the fluffiest socks she'd brought. She took off her thin wet ones and pulled them on. Cooper plugged in a space heater and Annabeth sat on the couch nearest its warm blowing air.

"I'm going to sit here and warm up a bit before bed, if that's okay."

"Whatever you want," he said. "I think I have some port if you'd like a little to help with the warming up. Or whiskey."

Annabeth usually wasn't much of a drinker, but the two glasses of wine with dinner had helped take the tense edge off. One more couldn't hurt. "Port would be great."

A minute later, Cooper brought two glasses back to the couch and sat next to her. Whatever his reason for sitting so close, Annabeth told herself it was because of the space heater.

"Cheers," she said and they clinked glasses.

"Cheers," he repeated. "So, I have an idea. I'm not sure you're going to like it, but I want you to hear me out."

Curious but cautious, she asked, "What?"

"Tomorrow's Friday," he started. "I have a computer I keep out here because I come out most weekends. It's set up so I can log into the system at Paws. As the director, obviously, I have access to every part of the system, including finance. So, what would you think about working from here tomorrow?"

Annabeth thought about it. It wasn't a terrible idea, though it wasn't great, either. All of her notes were at the office as well as printouts she'd been referring to. Even so, there was enough other stuff to do that she could make it work. She wasn't sure why he thought she wouldn't like the idea. Then it dawned on her.

"You have just the one computer?"

"Yes," he said.

"We both can't work on it at the same time," she said, though she really didn't have to.

"No, we can't. Here's the thing. I have a meeting with the board of directors. I've been gone for two months, so I cannot reschedule it. I was thinking you'd work here and I'd go into the office."

He was right. She didn't like his idea at all.

Before she could express this, he said, "Look, after last night—even if he didn't mean for us to see him—we learned the guy isn't afraid of firing that gun. And for whatever reason, you are his target. No one knows you're here, which means you are absolutely safe. Plus, Rusty is just down the road."

His logic was sound but, now, after the guy finding Cooper with her not once, but twice, she worried he could be a target as well. But she knew there'd be no talking him out of staying, with his meeting with board members on the calendar.

"It's really not appropriate for me not to be at work. I'm a new employee."

"New employees get sick just like the rest of us. I'll tell everyone you took a sick day. Besides, I'd rather risk a little tarnish on your reputation than bullets flying at your head."

"That's overly dramatic," Annabeth said, finishing the last of her nightcap. "I don't think it's necessary, but as long as I can get some work done, I'll stay behind."

Cooper finished his drink and took both glasses to the kitchen. "I'm glad. I'm going to put you in my room because it has the bigger bed." Before she could tell him it wasn't necessary, and she'd inconvenienced his life enough as it was without taking his bed too, he added, "And don't argue with me about it. Bring the space heater. That way you can close the bedroom door."

"What about you? You'll be cold."

"I'll be fine. With Brody's bedroom door open, I'll be plenty warm. It's already much warmer."

They said good night and Annabeth found herself alone in his bedroom.

~ * ~

The next morning, without intending to, Annabeth didn't wake until after 9:00. Of course, she found herself alone in the cabin. Like the morning in her apartment, Cooper left a note about the coffee being pre-made. She pushed the "on" button. He left a second note instructing her to check the stove every couple of hours, adding extra logs as need. He left a third note in the form of a Post-it on his computer monitor with instructions for getting into the Paws network.

She knew she should get dressed, but decided to enjoy the luxury of working in her flannel pjs and fluffy socks. She buzzed along for 90 minutes, only getting up once to refill her coffee cup. At 11:00, she logged out of the financial program and logged onto email. Nothing exciting, but she answered a few so as not to fall behind. Then she checked her voice mail with the remote access information she'd been given when she first started the job.

Only one. Finally. She learned a Detective Mitchell Jones had been assigned her case from Tuesday. It seemed so long ago, that first night when she'd been held at gunpoint. So much had happened since then. He left a number and asked her to please call him.

Annabeth mentally ran through the message she intended to leave Detective Jones as she dialed and heard the first ring. But, before the second ring, she heard, "Jones."

"Detective Jones," she stammered a bit. "This is Annabeth Neilson. Returning your call."

"Neilson. Yes. Hold, please," he said. He certainly wasn't one for pleasantries, Annabeth thought. "Okay," he said when he returned. "I needed your file."

He explained how he'd been assigned her case and apologized for the delay in following up. He said he had been in court the last couple days on two other cases.

"I've read the patrol officers' reports, but I'd like to go over what happened again with you in person, if possible."

Annabeth explained that she was out of town at the moment and agreed to see him first thing on Monday morning. But, she added, a few other incidents had happened since the initial one.

"Okay, I still want to see you Monday, but since I have you on the phone, why don't we go over everything so I can take some notes and get caught up? Let's start with the incident on Tuesday evening."

Annabeth sucked in a big breath and told the story of Tuesday. Jones interrupted several times to ask questions. Then she moved on to finding her office riffled through on Thursday morning. Annabeth assumed it was the gunman back looking for whatever he hadn't found Tuesday evening, but she couldn't prove it was him.

"Was anything missing?" the detective asked.

"No, not as far as I could tell."

"Okay, anything else?"

Annabeth steeled herself to relay the final incident, since she assumed he was going to give her an earful about not calling the police right away, since shots had been fired.

He listened intently, asking questions throughout her story. When she got to the part about the man firing at Cooper, Annabeth could almost hear him sit up straighter. But he surprised her by not berating her when she apologized for not calling 911 the night before. She also included that she left a message for Officer Weir as that was the only phone number she had.

He agreed the apartment needed to be photographed. He added that they might dust for fingerprints in a few places, but it sounded like they wouldn't yield anything.

Even though she started the call by saying she was out of town, the detective asked if she was safe. She didn't really want to say she was staying with her boss because she didn't want to give him the wrong impression, but she wasn't about to lie to the police either. Trying to make it clear Cooper was only trying to protect her, Annabeth explained that she was staying at Cooper's cabin and she would remain at the cabin for the next couple days. Probably until their appointment on Monday.

"And I assume you locked your apartment before you left," Jones asked.

"Of course," she said, fighting hard not to add a Homer Simpson "d'oh" to the end.

"Okay. If you prefer, we can send a unit to your apartment after our meeting on Monday. It's not ideal, but since you are out of town and the place is secure, it should be fine," he said. "Speaking of Mr. Cooper, I'll also need to talk to him. Could you arrange for him to come with you on Monday, or should I call him myself?"

"Thank you. I would prefer to do it Monday. Yes, I think I can arrange for Cooper—Mr. Cooper—to come with me. I mean, I'm not sure what's on his schedule but I'll try. If he can't make it, I'll have him call you to make his own appointment."

"Very good," he said. "In the meantime, I'll see if anyone reported those gunshots last night and ask the watch sergeant to have a patrol car drive by your apartment a couple times each shift if they can."

"I appreciate it, Detective," Annabeth said. He told her to call anytime and reminded her to not hesitate to call 911 if she saw the gunman again.

After they disconnected, Annabeth called Cooper's cell phone. When he didn't answer, she assumed he was in the meeting with the board members, though she couldn't remember that he'd ever mentioned the time of the meeting. She left a message, letting him know she'd talked to Detective Jones and about their appointment on Monday morning. She left Jones's phone number in case he couldn't attend.

Annabeth found it difficult to get her mind back to her work. After that long conversation about everything that happened, her head was swimming again with questions. The same questions since Tuesday.

Even though they'd pretty much ruled it out, she still kept hearing the gunman say something about money, which brought her back to the Paws' finances.

A knock on the cabin door startled her so much, she actually cried out.

"It's Rusty," she heard through the door.

Annabeth opened the door and a swoosh of cold air whirled into the room. "Brr," she said. "Come in." Rusty entered and Moose followed. Annabeth patted the dog's head as he strolled by on his way to the stove where he lay down.

"I came to check on you."

"Thank you. I'm fine. No bad guys today," she said, trying to make light of the situation.

"Did you call the police?" he asked.

"Just got off the phone with them," she was happy to be able to report.

"Good. I'm heading to town to run some errands and wanted to make sure you'd be okay."

Annabeth's thoughts went back to the finances and she suddenly had an idea. Long shot, like every other idea so far, but still a new idea. "I'm going with you," she said.

"No," he said, as if she were asking permission.

"I'm going with you," she said more firmly. "You can drop me off in midtown. There's a coffee shop across the street from where I'm going. I'll go there after I'm done to wait for you. When you finish your errands, you can swing by and pick me up. It'll be fine. I'll buy you a coffee. No one will know I'm there."

Rusty walked across the cabin to the stove. He opened the door and started stuffing logs into it.

"Stop, what are you doing?" Annabeth said. "You can't stop me by leaving the fire on."

He looked up at her. "This will be enough to burn for the next several hours. That way you'll still have coals by the time we get back." The black metal door squeaked as he closed it.

"Thank you."

"So, where are we going?"

"To see an old friend," Annabeth said, purposefully vague.

Seventeen

Glad to be done with the meeting with his board of directors, Cooper walked into the suite of offices of the Hewlett Building in midtown where Annabeth's former employer, Gibson & Gellar, took the entire fourth floor. In the large reception area, his eyes found Annabeth as she sat looking down, tugging on a thread of her coat. She looked nervous, unsteady. What the hell was she doing here?

"Can I help you?" a young male receptionist asked.

Annabeth looked up. Her eyes widened. "I'm with her," he said, pointing to Annabeth.

"Mr. Gibson shouldn't be much longer," the young man reported.

Cooper thanked him and joined Annabeth on one of three sofas in the highly-designed beige and black waiting area. He didn't speak, just quietly sat next to her.

For a full minute, she didn't say anything either. Then she asked under her breath, and without turning to face him, "What are you doing here?"

"The better question, I should think, is what are *you* doing here?"

"I'm fine. No one would think to look for me here."

"That wasn't the question. We agreed you'd stay out at the cabin," Cooper said.

"How'd you know I was here anyway?"

"Come on. You're smarter than that," Cooper breathed out. "I gave my brother one assignment. To keep an eye on you. Did you think for one minute he wasn't going to tell me? He called after you got out of the car, and waited in the parking lot until I arrived."

"He shouldn't have done that," she said.

"He's ex-military and lives by a code of leave-no-man-behind."

"I'm not a fallen soldier, I haven't been left behind and I'm not a man. I'm perfectly fine."

A group of three came around the corner from a back office talking and laughing. They left together out the front glass doors.

"You still haven't answered my question. What are you doing here? Trying to get your old job back?" It sounded petulant, but he couldn't help himself.

That got her attention. She whipped her head to look at Cooper, anger in her eyes and her lips pursed. "No. I'm not trying to get my old job back. If you must know, I decided to get the opinion of someone with more auditing experience. Contrary to the evidence and what I said before, I can't get this nagging feeling to go away. I still think the Paws' finances could be part of the equation. And I'd prefer to talk to Gil, Mr. Gibson alone."

Cooper didn't say anything for a minute. He didn't want to blurt out something rude, unprofessional or hurtful. He took a calming breath. "We're in this together. That's what we said. If this is about Paws' finances, then I'm going in. If this is something else, something personal, then we are leaving and you can do this another day."

"I'm not trying to get my old job back," she hissed at him. "Why would you even think that?"

Something just wasn't adding up for Cooper. If this really were about Paws, why hadn't she suggested this visit days earlier when they were thinking outside the box? Had she hated staying at his cabin so much that she was making up excuses to get out?

Before he could say anything more, Annabeth changed the subject. "Did you get my message about the detective? Did anyone say anything about me not being at the office?"

"Yes. And, no, not really. Shannon asked where you were, and I said you weren't feeling well. Zoey mentioned you two were supposed to get together to talk about the year-end fundraising goals and strategy."

"Darn it. I completely forgot about the meeting with Zoey."

"She said it was fine and that you could talk Monday."

"My day planner is at work," she said, to further explain the lapse.

"It's fine," he repeated.

He still wanted to talk more about what was really going on. Before he formed the right words, a woman entered the waiting area. She was impeccably dressed in a yellow and orange dress with a yellow print scarf tied at her neck and simple pearl earrings, her hair, pulled back into a tight high bun.

"Annabeth," the woman said.

"Darcy." Annabeth stood and hugged the woman lightly. "It's good to see you. How have you been?"

"Sorry for the long wait. Mr. Gibson was on an international call."

"No worries. I didn't have an appointment, so I'm just happy he was able to squeeze me in."

"For you? Always. Come on back." The woman turned and they followed her around the corner and down a long hallway until they reached the corner of the building to the office with the large brass plate engraved with *Gilbert T. Gibson, Partner*. Below that was a string of letters including CPA and MBA and several Cooper didn't recognize.

The double doors were closed and Darcy knocked lightly. Without waiting for a response, she opened the door. Annabeth and Cooper followed. The woman turned to the pair and asked if she could get them anything to drink. Coffee? Water?

Cooper spoke for both of them when he said, "No, thank you." But he did so without looking at Darcy. He couldn't take his eyes off Annabeth intensely looking at Mr. Gibson intensely looking back at Annabeth, so much being communicated without a word being spoken. Cooper just wished he knew what exactly it meant. He was pretty sure neither had blinked since they'd stepped into the large office. He was irritated and—what?—jealous, maybe. No, that couldn't be it, he thought.

Gibson, a good looking salt-and-pepper haired man in his 50s, was dressed in an expensive, well-tailored black suit that he wore with a blinding-white shirt and a solid red tie. Slick was the word that came to mind as Cooper waited to be introduced.

Gibson came around his mammoth-sized mahogany desk with open arms as if to embrace Annabeth, but she stuck out her arm making it clear they'd only be shaking hands. Cooper was glad for that.

"We miss you around here," Gibson said, holding on to her hand long after they shook.

Annabeth turned toward Cooper. "Gil Gibson, this is Malcolm Cooper, the director at Rescued Paws where I work now."

Cooper reached out to grasp Gibson's extended hand. He told himself not to squeeze too hard. There was nothing to prove and he didn't want to appear petty, though he certainly felt that way toward this man he didn't even know.

"Pleased to meet you. Sit down," Gibson said. He returned behind his desk while Annabeth and Cooper took seats in wide leather chairs across from him. "Annie, it's great to see you, of course. But this isn't a social call, is it?" he asked.

Annie?

Cooper wasn't sure how much she was going to share with the this man. First, she ignored the statement about how pleased he was to see her. Then, she downright surprised Cooper when she spun a tale with almost no truth. Annabeth was cool, professionally distant as she explained there had been some worry that the previous bookkeeper may have been doing some funny business when it came to Paws' money. She went on to explain the ways she'd tried to ferret out any wrongdoing but reported she had come up empty-handed.

"So, the reason we came," she concluded, surprising Cooper that she included him, since she was angry he had showed up in the first place. "We want to pick your brain, to see if you had any ideas we could pursue. Financially speaking."

Gibson listened as she spoke and when she finished, he leaned back in his big executive chair and looked to the ceiling in thought.

He sat upright again and looked at Annabeth. "Annabeth, you're a good accountant. I know you focused on taxes while you were here, but even so, I'm inclined to think if there were something to find, you'd find it. But, just in case, let me throw out a few things."

"Please," Annabeth said.

"Did you take a look at the assets? Things like equipment? A person could hide wrongdoing there. You know, depreciate an asset over a long period of time so it would have little effect on the bottom line from month-to-month. That could easily go unnoticed. Of course, you'd have the cash outlay at the onset, but still worth looking at, I'd think."

Annabeth reached across Gibson's desk and helped herself to a blank sheet of paper from a pad with the company's black and tan logo as though she'd done it a hundred times before. She then looked around his desk. Gibson opened his top drawer a couple inches, retrieved a pen and handed it to her.

Cooper was struck by the level of familiarity. He got the impression she'd sat across this desk many times before. Cooper chided himself. First, he wasn't going to get petty. Second, of course she'd sat across the desk. Hadn't she worked in this office for 10 or 12 years?

Annabeth scribbled a few notes. "What else?" she asked. "Anything. Even a long shot."

"Okay, this is along the same lines but, if it were me and, as you indicated, nothing was obvious, I'd do a complete inventory check. Maybe you paid for inventory that you don't actually own."

"Good," Annabeth said, adding to her notes.

"Even though it can be tedious, I'd do a thorough check into your vendors. Your instinct was good to check to see if they had business licenses on file with the State of Alaska, but go further. Look at the owners of those licenses because anyone can get one. It's just a matter of paying a fee, having a bank account and filling out a form."

She looked up from her notetaking. "Yeah, I thought of that one. Just haven't had the time yet. Anything else?"

"The only other thing—and this is so obvious I'm sure you already considered it—hire a forensic accountant. Rescued Paws is small enough that it won't cost an arm and a leg, though it won't be cheap either."

"How much would something like that run?" Cooper asked.

"What does your regular annual audit cost you, Malcolm?"

"About ten thousand dollars, maybe a little more," Cooper answered.

"Then, I'd guess double that for a specialty audit. We don't do them here, so you'd have to ask to be sure, but I think twenty thousand would put you in the ballpark. They'll have to look deep into the minutiae of your books if you, Annabeth, or your regular auditors haven't found anything."

Cooper tried keeping his face impassive and not register the sticker shock. There was simply no way Paws could afford something like that, especially considering this was all speculation to begin with. There was no way to prove the tall man's visits had anything to do with the finances of Rescued Paws.

"Annabeth," Gibson said. "It goes without saying you must do your due diligence for your organization. You must disclose your concern to both your auditors and your board of directors, if you haven't already. Don't go this alone." Then he looked at Cooper. "Don't let her. She absolutely cannot risk her CPA license by ignoring it. You only have to watch the news to know financial improprieties are not to be taken lightly. Someone later might find something, and then there'd be incompetence accusations to deal with. She's too good to take those type of risks or to have something like this follow her through her career."

Cooper agreed. It was obvious Gibson cared about Annabeth. He offered solid suggestions (as near as Cooper could tell) and was looking out for her, professionally-speaking.

He continued, "Even if you are a nonprofit and cannot afford a forensic accountant, it sounds to me like you cannot afford not to get one."

Cooper stood and Gibson followed. "Thank you," Cooper said reaching out to shake his hand across the giant desk. He wanted to dislike the guy, but it was hard not to see his genuine concern for

Annabeth and, by extension, Paws. "We appreciate your taking the time."

"Anything for Annabeth," he said. "If it comes to that and you truly cannot afford one, give me a call. Maybe I can call in a favor and get you a 'friends' discount."

"Thank you," Cooper said, hating the idea of letting the guy do him a favor. But, if it came to pass, he might not have a choice. "I appreciate it. We'll let you know."

Annabeth stood and Gibson said, "Annie, could we have a word in private?"

Cooper was caught like an animal in a cage for a moment. It took a second for him to say, "Annabeth and I are working together on this, so anything you have to say to her, you can say in front of me."

Mr. Gibson looked intently at Cooper, his professionalism never wavering. Then he looked back to Annabeth, who remained quiet, though she did not avert her eyes from him. She nodded to Gibson, affirming what Cooper said.

Gibson was taken aback and it showed ever so slightly. Cooper was pretty sure he wasn't used to hearing the word no, even when couched in polite, professional conversation. But he quickly gained his composure and said, "Okay. Malcolm, I wanted to tell her that just because you are helping her on this project, it doesn't mean she shouldn't take a thorough look at your financial activities as well. Next to the finance person, a CEO is the most likely to—shall we say—mismanage funds."

Cooper knew he was clean, but an outsider wouldn't. He hated that Gibson's advice was sound, though wholly untrue.

Annabeth nodded in acknowledgement.

"And, Annabeth, I also want to say that you were a valuable asset to the Gibson & Gellar team. You're well regarded here and among the clients you worked with. In other words, you always have a place here. Just say the word."

Was Gibson trying to poach her right in front of him? Cooper wondered.

Annabeth said she appreciated his kind words. She shook his hand and this time Cooper could see her hand softening in his.

Gibson walked them to his door and they said goodbye again. He closed the door behind them.

As they waited for Cooper's truck to warm, Cooper looked over at Annabeth. She definitely wasn't angry anymore. What was she? If he didn't know better, he'd almost say she was sad. Defeated. Clearly, something had gone on during that meeting that had nothing to do with the financial concerns of Paws.

He knew he risked truly angering her which, in turn, risked shutting her down, but Cooper felt like he needed to say it. "You know what I think? I think you knew Rusty would call me and I'd come here."

She turned to him, blinking rapidly. "That's not true." She blinked a few more times. "Well, uh, I don't know. If that's true, it wasn't conscious. I swear. But maybe you're right. I had no business coming here."

"Well, I wouldn't say that. You took notes. That must mean Gibson offered some ideas of things we haven't yet tried."

"Mr. Gibson, Gil, is the reason I left the firm."

Eighteen

Blinking no longer could contain her emotions and tears rolled from her eyes as soon as she said it. It was the first time she'd said it out loud. *Gil was the reason I left the firm.* She had felt so humiliated and going back to Gibson & Gellar had only made it worse. What was wrong with her? She truly thought it a sound idea when it occurred to her in the cabin after Rusty said he was coming into town.

She owed Cooper an explanation. He deserved that, but she struggled to find the words to explain it to him when, even now that she was no longer in the middle of it, she still found it hard to explain to herself.

"I told Rusty I'd call him," Cooper said, fishing his phone from his pants pocket. Annabeth knew, and appreciated, that while it probably wasn't true, what he was really doing was giving her time to get herself together.

"Rusty, hey. Yeah, everything's fine. I have Annabeth, so you don't need to come back here. I need to stop at the office for a bit and then we'll head out to the cabin. She's fine. It's accounting stuff, so I'll let Annabeth explain when we see you. Sounds good. I don't feel much like cooking tonight so would you pick up Thai food? Get five or six different things and we'll share. Annabeth's vegetarian, so be sure at least a couple of them don't have any meat. Oh, wait, hold on—"

Cooper turned to Annabeth and said, "I should've asked before I called. Do you like Thai food?"

She smiled through her tears. He definitely was not like Gil. "Love it," she said.

"And it's okay tonight for dinner?"

"It's perfect."

"Any requests?"

She shook her head. Then added, "Well, I can't do four-chili spicy."

Cooper smiled and put the phone back up to his ear. "No heat on the vegetarian dinners." He listened. Annabeth could hear Rusty's voice but couldn't make out the words. "Okay, I need to stop for wine, anyway. No, I won't forget the beer."

Cooper disconnected and returned the phone to his pocket.

"All set."

The truck was beginning to warm, but Annabeth still didn't feel ready to talk about her past. "I guess we need to go to the office," she said.

"You dropped a pretty big bomb. Are we going to talk about it?"

She didn't know how to respond. Annabeth wished he could just know without her actually having to tell him.

"Later?" he finally said, offering her an easy out.

"Later."

Cooper put the truck in reverse and drove across town to Rescued Paws. "I need about an hour," he said. "Do you want to come in? Or, if you're more comfortable, I can leave the truck on and you can stay here. The gas tank is more than three-quarters full."

"I'll come in. I have some notes in my office I'd like to get." Annabeth wiped her eyes, blew her nose and hoped, if she saw anyone inside, they'd chalk up the red and puffiness of her face to the cold.

In the building, Cooper headed to his office. Before Annabeth went to hers, she went to the intake desk and asked yet a different volunteer about Solstice. More often than not, when you ask two different people the same question, you get two different answers. The little black dog had streamed in and out of her mind since she had first met her two days earlier. Each time she thought about the puppy's sweet face with the white angel kiss above her eye, she felt more certain there was a reason she'd ducked into the drop-off room that day. She was meant to meet that particular dog and, dare she say, become her human mama.

Annabeth wasn't ready to give up on the idea that Solstice was gone, returned to a family or otherwise.

The volunteer today, unlike most, was young, probably Annabeth's age. Annabeth approached the desk and made small talk for a minute before going through the same explanation and questions she had the day before with Stanley.

Unfortunately in this case, the two volunteers gave the exact same answer. No record of a Lab dropped off any day during the week. No record of a puppy getting assigned a foster family or adopted. No record of a family claiming a lost dog.

"Hey, lady. What are you doing here?" she heard a woman's voice behind her. Annabeth didn't even notice that Shannon had come to the desk, focused as she was on her discussion with the volunteer.

"Oh, hi. You startled me."

"Sorry. Usually you can hear me coming from a mile away, but it's Friday." The translation of this statement was that, most days, Shannon wore high heels that clicked and clacked as she walked through the office since only the individual offices were carpeted because dogs and carpet were not a good combination. And if one listened closely, you could often also hear tingly sounds from the dangly earrings she adored. Today, though, was casual Friday and Shannon had decided to go all-in on her Christmas-themed ensemble. She wore a red pleated skirt and green knit sweater with a holiday wreath. Big green shiny bauble earrings shaped like Christmas ornaments hung from each ear. Her legs were warmed with black tights and, on her feet she wore a pair of red Keds sneakers. The shoes were an odd choice, Annabeth thought, because she was confident Shannon owned more than one pair of red heels. "So, what are you doing here? Cooper said you were sick. You didn't come to infect all of us, did you?" Shannon laughed at her own joke.

"I'll keep my distance," Annabeth assured her, coming up with a plausible explanation. "I'm feeling a little better now, but I didn't want to get behind, so thought I'd pick up a few things and work on them at home over the weekend."

"Sick days are for when you're sick, silly. You don't have to make them up. I'm sure Cooper doesn't expect you to."

"I know, thanks. I'm still new and I don't want to get behind," she said again.

"Shannon," the volunteer cut in, "Do you know anything about a black Lab puppy coming in this week?"

Shannon looked to the volunteer, then back to Annabeth. "This is the same puppy we talked about yesterday, I assume?" Annabeth could see Shannon was a little irritated that Annabeth wouldn't drop it. Shannon was probably nervous about getting in trouble for one of her volunteers not following the proper protocol, costing the organization precious income. "No, still don't know anything. I really think its owner came in and claimed it. And we just didn't put it in the system."

Annabeth thought about asking if there were any new dogs. But even though she had just met the black Lab, it was going to take a day or two to get her head around the fact that Solstice might not be an option for her first dog.

Annabeth asked if Zoey were still around but learned she had left early for a meeting with her first grader's teacher. Their meeting would have to wait until Monday.

"Well, then, I better grab what I need and get out of here. You two have a nice weekend," Annabeth said.

They told her to do the same, then Shannon added, "Don't forget, Monday afternoon we deck the halls. Well, the lobby. Should be fun and festive. Simon said he'll bring eggnog and I thought I may bake cookies this weekend."

Annabeth thanked her for the reminder because, truth was, she had forgotten employees were going to spend a couple hours putting up holiday decorations. She wondered how long it would take for the police to fingerprint and photograph her apartment after the meeting with Detective Jones.

In her office, Annabeth sat at her desk. She had forty minutes to kill before Cooper would be ready, assuming an hour was all he needed to wrap up the week. She certainly hadn't made his first week back an easy one. Annabeth guessed she'd cut his productivity by half while they chased their tails. Maybe more. Probably more. She was sorry for that and hoped next week would be less distracting. One could hope, right?

Annabeth turned on her computer and logged into the financial system. She printed out a detailed inventory report as well as the details of their assets. She might have been sorry she had gone to see Gil, but she had to admit, he knew the job. He provided ideas she hadn't yet thought of.

Because she was so new, the printouts might not be of use out at Cooper's cabin, since she wasn't familiar with all the equipment, furniture and other items on the depreciation schedule around the office. But it couldn't hurt to start looking and making notes, and Cooper might be able to help.

As her printer spit out the lengthy reports, Annabeth thought again about Solstice. Then about dogs in general. The more she let the idea settle into her bones, into her heart, the more she felt a dog was exactly what she needed. Mentally, she added to her to-do list. Look online for houses with yards for rent.

The printer stopped after the last page. She gathered the stack and secured the pages with a large binder clip. The only other things she wanted to bring were the notes she'd written from the previous days as she'd studied the financials.

Even though she'd been in the office for a half hour, it suddenly felt like something was off. Again. Hadn't she closed her notebook the last time she left the office? She searched her memory to find the last time she'd been in the office. Yes, she was almost certain she'd closed it.

Annabeth closed her eyes and put her elbows on her desk. She rested her face in her hands. She messaged her temples and then her entire forehead. Surely, she was just being paranoid. After all, the office had already been gone through once, presumably without the person finding what he was looking for. Why would he go through it again? Whatever he was looking for clearly wasn't within these four walls.

"You're losing it," she said aloud. Annabeth shut the notebook with a decisive thud and added it to the bound reports. It was time to get out of there.

Just in case, she thought, on the off chance she wasn't paranoid, Annabeth took out her phone and snapped a dozen photos of her office and desk. If something looked skewed on Monday, she'd be able to point to the photos to prove it wasn't all in her head.

Nineteen

Instead of working as he should've been, Cooper sat at his desk thinking about Annabeth. She'd been so reckless by leaving the safety of his cabin to visit Gibson & Gellar. Why? And what did Gibson really want to say to her if Cooper had agreed to leave the two of them alone at the end of the meeting?

Cooper suspected she hadn't left Gibson & Gellar for professional reasons. If there had been problems with her work or she'd left on bad terms, Annabeth wouldn't have received the reception she had from either Gibson or his assistant. Both seemed genuinely glad, albeit surprised, to see her. And even though he hadn't been around when Rescued Paws hired her, Cooper knew the board of directors' executive committee would've diligently checked her references and, considering how long she had been at Gibson & Gellar, it would've been the most important one.

He shook his head. *Stop thinking about her. Work.* How many hours had he lost this week? And, this, his first week back after two months. There was so much to do. At least he could catch up some at the cabin this weekend.

His cozy cabin all weekend long, just him and Annabeth. He had to admit, he liked the idea. But the idea, no doubt, was more romantic than the reality. His time would be spent working. And she both told him and showed him that she had no interest in him. Still, she would be there and that was a nice thought.

Work, he told himself again.

Cooper shot off two dozen emails in quick succession. Then spent a little more time on a lengthy email to the board members as a follow-up to their morning meeting regarding filling an empty board seat, a February event, and the new flooring that was so desperately needed throughout the building, an expense they had hoped to put off for two years, but that Cooper wanted to convince them couldn't wait that long. His goal was new flooring by summer.

When he gathered the entire foot high stack of papers from his in-box, it was ambitious, he knew, but he decided to err on the side of optimism. Before he'd left to be with his mother, it was several inches and had only gotten higher in the weeks of his absence. If he could get through everything this weekend at the cabin, he'd happily call that a win.

A glance at his wall clock told him to hurry. He wanted to leave in the next ten minutes. He always tried to leave town before 4:00 on Fridays. If he couldn't, then he'd wait around until after 6:00 to avoid that harrowing window when everyone else was getting off work and leaving town for the weekend.

He went to the warehouse, where things were quiet, and retrieved a flat-bottomed reusable grocery bag with the Rescued Paws logo. Then back at his office, he attempted to put the entire paper stack, including the box, into the bag. The sides kept collapsing, making it difficult.

"Let me help," he heard Annabeth's sweet voice behind him. He felt her come up behind him and held open the bag so the box and its tall stack of loose papers slid right in. "Lucky I came along when I did," she said.

"Lucky."

"I came to see if you were on schedule or if you needed more time."

"On time. In fact, I'm pretty much ready. You?"

"Same. Can I have the keys to your truck? I'll go out there now and wait. Just so people don't see us leave together. I really don't want people thinking things they shouldn't be thinking."

The song "Let's Give Them Something to Talk About" popped into his head. *Where did that come from?* He refrained from saying it out loud and instead said, "Good idea." He fished his keys from the pocket of his jeans and dropped them into her palm. "Go ahead and start it, would you?"

"Of course. I'll see you out there."

Cooper watched after her until she closed the door behind her. Again, he thought he didn't care about the fact he had to work all weekend or that she wasn't interested in him, he simply enjoyed being in her presence. Yes, kissing her would be nice. More than nice. But it wasn't necessary to enjoy the time spent together.

Feeling even more optimistic and gleeful than he had before she came into the room, Cooper added the hundred pieces or more of the unopened mail that had accumulated in his absence to the grocery bag. By the time he was done, the bag had some heft to it.

Before he left, Cooper stopped at the intake desk to tell the volunteer thank you. He tried to remember to do that with some regularity. Rescued Paws would be lost without the thousands upon thousands of hours volunteers gave the organization every year. He poked his head into Shannon's office to say goodnight. Then went down the hall to Zoey's office, but it was dark. That was okay; he had already sent an email to let her know they needed to talk after the weekend about the upcoming fundraising campaign and the February event. Simon, the facility manager, and other staff were technically full-time but only worked 32 hours a week so most chose not to work on Fridays.

It was nice getting into an almost-warm truck. "Ready?" he asked Annabeth.

"Yep," she said. They stopped about halfway to the cabin at a liquor store. Cooper ran in and emerged with a 12-pack of Alaskan Amber beer in its distinct red box. He put it in the bed of the truck, then returned and emerged a second time with a case of wine.

"How much do you think we're going to drink?" Annabeth laughed when he got in the truck.

"I know it looks bad." He joined in laughing. "I try to keep a little stock on hand out there and that port we drank was the last of it. I've been meaning to stock up for a while. Since we had to stop, I figured it was as good a time as any."

"Should we get snowed in, we won't perish. We'll pickle."

"What could be better?" he laughed. Unfortunately for him, snow was not forecast over the weekend.

After they arrived at the cabin and unloaded, Cooper tucked a flashlight into his coat pocket and the pair walked back along the road to Rusty's cabin. Inside, Cooper bent to add a few logs to Rusty's stove. As he did so, he asked Moose if he needed to go outside.

He heard Annabeth laugh behind him. He straightened and looked around. Moose was already gone. Cooper laughed. "I guess he's taking himself for a walk."

Even so, after Cooper closed the door to the stove, they left the cabin and continued to walk down the road. Cooper called to Moose every few minutes until the dog joined them. Even though the sun had set a couple hours earlier, the full-sky overcast bounced enough light that he didn't need to use the flashlight. The walk was peaceful and Cooper loved the calm feeling that overcame him. If only he could hold onto it. At least for the weekend.

Near the end of the road, the threesome turned around and went back the way they came. First, Moose ran to the door of Rusty's cabin, but after Cooper called to him a few times, he reluctantly joined them for the walk to Cooper's.

"Your daddy will be back soon," Annabeth explained to the dog as they came to Cooper's cabin. Inside, the dog, somewhat begrudgingly, went to his place by the stove, though he didn't seem to settle.

They couldn't have planned it better if they tried, because not fifteen minutes later, Rusty walked through the door with two white grocery bags of food. The smell filled the room. Moose went a little crazy with excitement to see his dad. After a few pets and another trip outside, Moose curled up near the stove.

One food bag included paper plates, little packets of soy sauce, and Thai sweet chili sauce, and a big stack of napkins. Cooper got forks and serving spoons. The food had stayed surprisingly hot, despite the more than 90-minute drive from town. Rusty hadn't been as lucky as Cooper and Annabeth. He got stuck in the harrowing Friday night after-work traffic window so was slowed considerably.

Cooper opened a bottle of beer and put it in front of his brother, then brought a bottle of red wine and an opener to the table. Rusty grabbed both and uncorked the wine while Cooper found two wine glasses.

"You're two peas in a pod," Annabeth said as Rusty poured the first glass and handed it to her.

"We are not," Rusty said. "What does that even mean?"

"I have no idea," Cooper said, laughing and taking his wine from his brother.

Over dinner, Annabeth did her best to explain in laymen's terms the leads Gibson had suggested and how wrongdoing could be hidden in those line items. Cooper grasped it more than Rusty, since he'd been hearing about the financials for eight years, ever since he took the job as director of Rescued Paws. But his grasp on what she was talking about was iffy at best. Even so, he loved how confidently she spoke when she was in her element. She had a way of making accounting and company financials sexy, which was something Cooper never imagined possible.

Toward the end of the meal, when Rusty and Cooper finally agreed that hearing her explain yet again would not deepen their understanding, Annabeth said, "Oh, and I forgot. There was one bit I figured out this morning. Not related to assets or inventory or depreciation."

"Bring it on," Rusty said, toasting the air with his third beer.

She turned to Cooper. "Do you remember when we were talking to Maggie?"

"Sure," Cooper replied.

"Just before we left, she tossed out that she had noticed a decline in pet adoptions starting about three years ago."

"I remember. Since that wasn't really about money, we dismissed it. Right?"

"Right. And it's still likely dismissible, but I did verify it's true. Three years ago, there was a downturn in adoptions. I didn't notice it when I was looking before because adoption fees make up such a small percentage of our overall budget."

Cooper cut in to interpret for Rusty. "We get most of our money from grants, fundraising, donations, etc. Not from the fees we charge people who adopt one of our animals. Those fees cover a small percentage of the total costs of food, vet visits, meds, vaccines, spay and neutering, and so on."

Rusty said, "I remember. I paid that fee when you found Moose for me."

"Exactly," Annabeth said. "Three years ago, as coincidence would have it, the annual Kitty Quilt Auction, a new fundraising event, started. It raises five thousand dollars or so, which is in the ballpark of the amount of a decrease we saw in adoption fees. So, when I was looking for anomalies on the bottom line—"

"There wasn't one," Cooper finished for her.

"Precisely."

"So, what does it mean?" Rusty asked.

Annabeth slouched in defeat. "Nothing. Probably nothing. At least not in terms of what's been happening. But I thought it was interesting. Maybe even worth looking into further. After three years, it's more than a blip. More than the natural ebb and flow. I'd need to look into it further to confirm, but I surmise we are seeing a trend where less pets are in need of a home."

"Which would be important for us to know for strategic planning, staffing, many things," he added.

"Some grants are based on the number of animals we serve, so if that number is truly trending down—and is not part of that ebb and flow cycle—we definitely need to prepare for that. The numbers weren't a dramatic drop three years ago, which is another reason it wasn't obvious. It's been a gradual and steady decline, nevertheless."

"We should look into that later. When we have time. When this other nonsense is figured out."

"Definitely," Annabeth agreed.

Rusty took a beer for the road, all 1/8 mile of it and said goodnight. He left the dishes for Cooper and Annabeth, since they'd left the ones the night before for him. He said he'd be back the next night for leftovers. He'd bought so much food, there was plenty for a full meal a second time over.

Cleanup took all of five minutes.

"How about a glass of port? I don't have it very often, but last night it really hit the spot," Cooper said. "And we have a new bottle."

"It was good. Of course, I've already had two glasses of wine. You aren't trying to get me drunk, are you?"

That wasn't the kind of guy Cooper was, and he was pretty sure Annabeth knew that. He said, "Just trying to help you sleep."

"Sure, I'll have a nip," Annabeth said, smiling. Those dimples made her face light up. Those, and her blue eyes.

"Now, is that a real nip or a Maggie nip?" he teased.

"Hmm, maybe halfway between the two."

"Sit. Relax. I'll bring it out." Cooper used their same wine glasses from dinner as his cabin wasn't really set up for guests. Before last night, in fact, he'd never had anyone out for a visit except for an occasional hiking buddy. He poured a nip and a half into each glass and took them to the couch where Annabeth had gotten comfortable.

They were quiet for a while. Sipping the sweet thick wine. Listening to the crackle of wood burning in the stove.

Annabeth broke the silence. "I'm going to tell you something now," she said, her voice quivering.

Did he want to know? He did. And he didn't. And, really, he already knew. "You don't owe me an explanation. I know I wanted one in the moment outside Gibson & Gellar. But you really don't. Not unless it affects Paws in some way."

She smiled weakly. Eyes averted into her wine glass. "It doesn't have to do with Paws. At least not in any relevant way. I've never told this to anyone. Well, people know, but I've never told anyone."

"In the truck you said Gibson was the reason you left that job. Maybe start there," he offered.

"Yeah. It starts there. Ends there. And the entire story in between is there." She looked up and Cooper gave her a reassuring smile.

"You don't have to tell me," he said again.

"I'm thinking you already know. It's an old unoriginal story."

"I know. But I don't know *your* story," he said.

"I was a fool. It's such a cliché it's almost laughable. Except that it's my life, so it's not so laughable." She paused. "It started a year ago at a conference in Philadelphia." She paused again and took a sip. "It shouldn't have happened, because he was a partner. He wasn't my direct supervisor, so we managed to skip that cliché. But he was my department's head supervisor. In other words, he might not have been my boss, but he was my boss's boss. He was—is—thirty years older than me."

"Married?" Cooper asked, rounding out the old unoriginal story's cliché.

"Yes and no. I want you to know, I never would've started up with him if he were truly married. But, yes, technically he was. He was separated from his wife, and not in the slimy way men convince women they are separated when they really aren't. Their problems were gossip at the water cooler for years until finally they formally separated. They had separate houses, separate lives while they worked out the details of the divorce."

"Okay," Cooper said.

"I'll spare you all the gory details but fast forward to four months ago when I learned he and his wife decided to give it another go. He told me himself, and he told me before he moved back in with her. So, it wasn't slimy. He wasn't slimy."

Cooper waited.

"We'd been so careful around the office. No stolen glances. No secret touches. No lunches together. Nothing. I was so stupid to think no one knew. So stupid," she repeated.

"When it became clear that our breakup was fodder for my co-workers, I felt foolish, and so small. I just had to get out of there. There wasn't some big dramatic office blowup. Nothing like that. I just could no longer bear the looks on my co-workers' faces, the whispering. Gil begged me to stay and so did my department head. I was—I am—a good employee. I just couldn't be one at Gibson & Gellar any longer."

"You were humiliated and you'd had your heart broken," Cooper said.

Annabeth looked at him, an almost confused look on her face. "Humiliated, yes. I never thought about the other. I mean, don't get me wrong, we had a good thing and I was sad to see it end. But heartbroken? I don't know if I could say that."

"After almost a year together?"

"Well, eight months. You know, I guess I never gave it much thought. I always assumed his divorce would come through, but never once did I imagine or even fantasize it would mean that the two of us would get married. Maybe it was the age difference. I don't know. Don't get me wrong, I cared about him very much. Maybe even loved him, but I never saw Gil as my happily ever after. If there even is such a thing."

"I think there is. You'll find yours someday," Cooper promised.

"Was your wife yours?" Annabeth asked. "Happily ever after, I mean." Her question caught him off guard. They were supposed to be talking about her.

"I'm thirty-three years old," Cooper said. "I guess my hope for myself is that the love of my life is still in my future somewhere, because my future should be a lot longer than my past. I loved my wife very much when we first got married, but we had come to the end of the road. Or close to it, anyway. Then she died, so that part of our story never played out."

"I hope that for you, too," Annabeth said. "You know, what I just told you?"

"Yeah," Cooper replied.

"I want to tell you one more thing," she said.

Cooper couldn't imagine what it might be.

"The story I just told you is the reason why I couldn't let you redo the fast, less-than-memorable kiss in Whittier. I just cannot be that person again."

Twenty

Annabeth woke to sounds from the kitchen. Cooper was making a pot of coffee, she decided, and it made her smile despite the fact that last night had been her worst night of sleep since this whole thing started. She tossed and turned and tossed again, couldn't get comfortable. Couldn't get outside her own head.

Cooper had been nothing but kind and supportive when she explained her affair with Gil Gibson. Still, she felt—what was the word? Exposed? Vulnerable? In the night, she kept replaying the conversation with Cooper. Did she tell him too much? He'd offered her an out, told her that unless it was Paws related, she didn't have to tell. Maybe that was the better option. It was too late now.

Interspersed with yesterday's replays were images of the tall man pointing the gun at her, Cooper being shot at, Solstice licking her face, getting locked in the Whittier tunnel and pages and pages of numbers from the plethora of financial spreadsheets she'd reviewed in the last few days.

Annabeth debated trying to get a few more hours of sleep, but finally decided that, no matter how lethargic she felt, any attempt at sleep would likely have the same results as the previous eight hours.

She dragged herself out of bed and into the shower. Afterward, she felt better and a little more awake.

"Good morning," she said as she joined Cooper in the kitchen. "How long have you been up?"

"Not long."

"It looks like you've been at it for a while," Annabeth said and pointed to the kitchen table that Cooper had turned into a makeshift desk. His in-box sat on one corner of the table, but it didn't look like he'd even started on that. Even so, the rest of the table was covered in paper.

"It's deceptive. I could spin a big story about how much work I've managed to knock out this morning, but the truth is the only thing I've accomplished is to make piles of mail. Seventy percent of it is going to end up as fire starter, I'm sure, but I still have to go through it all. Toast?"

"Sure," Annabeth said.

"Or, I make pretty good scrambled eggs," he offered.

"Just toast, thanks."

Annabeth helped herself to a mug and poured coffee while she watched as he added four slices of thick bread to the toaster. He already had butter and a jar of homemade jam sitting out. "Refill?" Annabeth asked, looking around for his mug.

"Sure. Table."

She hadn't seen it at first, but then spotted the white mug camouflaged in front of the tall stack of white papers. She hated to think what would happen if a big wind came up.

The toaster made a pop sound and the bread jumped. Cooper put two slices on a plate and handed it to her. "I'll let you fix yours how you like. The jam is from Maggie. She gave a couple jars to everyone last Christmas. You know, I've been getting those two jars of jam every year since I started working at Paws. By any chance, did we include that in your job description? I really like my two jars of homemade jam."

Annabeth laughed. She helped herself to a thick layer of the raspberry spread. "So, is it okay if I work at your computer? It looks like you'll have your hands full here for a while," she said, pointing to the table.

"That's the plan. Although, as the boss, I feel like I must say that, since it's Saturday, there is no expectation that you work. I'm going to work, but you can play games if you want. Read. Relax."

"Thanks, but I think I'll work, too," she said.

Annabeth sat at the little desk with the computer on it in front of the window. Same as the day before. In the hint of the mid-morning sunrise, she could almost make out the silhouette of the cabin's surroundings. Snow. Pine trees. It was still mostly dark, since the sun came up so late in Alaska, especially this close to the winter solstice, the longest day of the year. She knew from yesterday that, at first light, she'd also be able to see a swatch of Rusty's cabin.

As the computer booted up, the black screen was like a mirror and she watched as Cooper got comfortable at the kitchen table behind her and picked up one of his mail stacks.

She was grateful it wasn't awkward this morning after a night of airing her dirty laundry. More grateful still that he hadn't brought up said laundry. He didn't treat her any differently. Outside of resisting her attraction to him, he was—plain and simple—a genuinely good guy. He was kind and generous and protective. She threw a mental wish out into the universe for him to find exactly what he hoped for himself last night. The love of his life. A romantic happily ever after. He deserved that. If it happened after she'd moved on from Paws, so much the better.

She checked email while she finished her toast. Replied to one. The others could wait until Monday.

There was so much of the day-to-day work that needed doing, but nothing sparked her interest. On the other hand, she'd spent so much time looking at the finances trying to figure out what the gunman had been talking about on Tuesday evening that doing more of the same felt like she'd just be spinning her wheels and she didn't feel like doing that this morning.

Finally, and despite the fact that the night before she said she'd look into it later, she decided to examine the adoption numbers. She opened a new spreadsheet and started by entering the income they'd made each month on fees over the past five years. It was only a little more detail than what she'd already discovered. She confirmed the gradual decrease had begun three years ago.

The finances really couldn't provide any more insight than that. She sat staring off into the trees she knew were out there, sipping her coffee. What next? She said she'd do a deeper dive, but what exactly was a deeper dive?

Then she got an idea. She remembered reading old packets that were put together each month for board members prior to their monthly meeting. It was during those first few weeks of employment when she was trying to get a handle on what was expected of her. And, of course, financials were a major component of those packets.

But so were other aspects of the agency. Shannon contributed a page on volunteer numbers and activities. Zoey wrote a report on fundraising efforts, as well as program information. The organization was too small to have a program manager, so it was Zoey who logged into the pet tracking system to gather information on program-related activities for the month.

Perhaps that's where she might find useful information. Annabeth put down her cup. She logged out of the financial system and clicked into all the shared files in a folder called "Board" and a subfolder called "Board Packets."

For the next two hours, she went methodically through each month for the past five years, extrapolating relevant data to add to her spreadsheet.

Twice during the morning, Cooper wordlessly came over and refilled her mug. And, once, after the sun had started its low trajectory over the sky, she nearly tumbled off her chair in fright when Moose whizzed by the cabin, a blur of black and brown fur. She looked up to catch him diving head first into a snow bank, then falling and rolling like a pig in mud. It made her smile. She wanted a dog who would frolic in the snow like that, then come back inside to snuggle her. Maybe she'd even frolic in the snow with her dog. Once she got a dog. Once she got a house where she could have a dog.

It was after one in the afternoon when she finished. She leaned back in the chair with an audible sigh.

"Does that mean you're ready for lunch?" she heard from behind.

She turned to see that Cooper had cleared the kitchen table of mail and, perhaps even started on the giant stack, the kindling box near the wood stove now filled with paper.

Annabeth offered to help, but Cooper insisted that she was his guest. So while he heated tomato soup and made grilled tri-cheese sandwiches, Annabeth stared at five years' worth of adoption data. She knew what she saw, what the data was telling her, but it took a while for it to really sink in because she knew it could detrimentally affect Paws.

When Cooper said lunch was ready, she stood. Sore from sitting so long in the wooden straight-back chair, she stretched her back and shoulders as she made her way to the kitchen table.

"Reminds me of being a kid," Annabeth said, looking at the grilled cheese sandwich and bowl of tomato soup.

"It reminds everyone of being a kid," Cooper laughed. "But it's so good. And fast. And easy. I've had this probably more than any other meal out here. Don't judge me."

She took a bite and with her mouth still full, she said, "I can see why. It is so good." Then added, "No judgment whatsoever." After she took a few more bites, chewed and swallowed, she said, "So, I know you said we'd look into this later, but I spent the morning trying to figure out the adoption numbers."

"And?"

"I don't quite know how to say it," she said tentatively.

"Just say it."

"It definitely looks like a trend. It's been a steady decline month after month, except for every January, interestingly enough, for the last three years."

"January is easy to explain. People give pets as gifts during the holiday season, mistakenly believing a pet makes a cute surprise. But often it's an unwelcomed surprise. So, spikes in January are, basically, gift returns."

"Makes sense. The bad thing about me only being in this business for only six—seven now—weeks is I just don't have the knowledge. The background."

"That's okay. We're a team, right? We complement each other. Anything else?"

"Yeah, two more things. First, it only seems to be affecting the canine numbers. Cat adoptions have, more or less, stayed steady. Second, I'd say eighty percent of the decrease in dog adoptions are puppies. For all intents and purposes, that other twenty percent is easily dismissed as the natural up and down. Bottom line? We have seen a steady decline in puppy adoptions over the last three years."

"Which actually means we're getting less puppies walking through our front door."

"True. Does that mean the spay and neutering program and PSAs are working? Does it mean less backyard breeders? What?"

"I don't know. The numbers are what they are. I can't dispute them, but something isn't sitting right with me. Only puppies? It's too clean. Too perfect. I don't know. I keep wondering what happened three years ago that triggered the decline."

"Good question," Annabeth agreed.

They wandered around a while longer with "what if" and "what about" ideas but nothing sparked. In the end, they agreed, for real this time, to put the problem on the back burner and revisit it after the new year, presumably after their other mystery was solved and the gunman was behind bars. Or at least stopped popping up.

After lunch, back at the computer desk, Annabeth had a hard time getting excited about work. It was Saturday, after all. She decided to call it a day on work and look for a house to rent.

Hours later, she had a dozen leads that were available beginning the first of January and, more importantly, that were in her price range. On Monday, she'd start making calls for appointments to view them. Thinking about a house with a yard for a dog filled her with happiness. She caught herself several times feeling a silly grin spread across her face. She probably looked ridiculous.

The final place she wanted to look before calling it a day was Craigslist. She was hesitant because she felt more comfortable going through a broker or an agency, or at least seeing a place listed on a more reputable site. But, at the same time, she knew people who'd found real gems through Craigslist.

It was slim pickings, probably the time of year. What Alaskan wanted to move in snow and cold and dark? It took only half an hour to go through the list and only one made it into the notebook. Even then, she followed it with a question mark.

Cooper was still hard at work behind her. Not that there was any rule that said she needed to keep working as long as he did. Though, she knew, you couldn't call what she was doing work. Still, she decided she'd sit another half hour before calling it a day.

On impulse, she clicked over to see the pets listed on Craigslist. It was practically heresy for a person working at a rescue group to get a pet from anywhere but their own organization. She was just looking, she told herself.

To be honest, her heart wasn't really in it. First, she needed to secure a house and, despite going through the dog listings, she knew she'd only seriously consider a Rescued Paws dog.

The next profile came up and Annabeth involuntary cried out, "No!"

Cooper was by her side in a split second as she pointed at the screen.

"What? What am I looking at?" he asked, desperate to understand what upset her so.

"That's Solstice!"

Twenty-one

Annabeth's breathing became ragged. She was nearly panting and was so visibly shaken from the imagine of the dog on the computer screen, Cooper actually thought about offering her a paper bag to breath into. He guided her to the couch and sat her down. Of course, he was curious what she was talking about, but none of that mattered at the moment with her on the verge of hyperventilating.

"Deep breaths," he said. "Calm down." She leaned forward over her knees. Cooper rubbed her back. Slow gentle circles. After a minute, her breathing slowed. She sat upright and crossed her hands over her chest, over her heart as if it needed comfort, too.

"Can you talk?" he asked.

She nodded.

"What just happened?"

She started by telling him the lease on her apartment was up at the end of the month, which he already knew since she'd mentioned it on their drive to Whittier. He hadn't thought much about it, since she also said it was probably too late and she'd likely renew the lease. Maybe something had changed. Still, none of this explained what had upset her.

"So, I was looking at rental properties," she said. Her breathing sped up once again, short staccato in breaths and out breaths. "Then I clicked over to look at dogs. I was just looking, I promise," she pleaded with him.

"It's okay," he reassured her.

"That's when it came up," she said pointing across the room to the image still on the screen.

Cooper shook his head. He still didn't get it.

"You remember that day in the drop-off room? When you came in and I was petting that black puppy?"

"Sure."

"You let me name it," she reminded him.

"Right. You chose Solstice."

"Precisely. I didn't tell you this, but I was thinking about adopting her. That's why I was looking at houses." Again, she pointed to the computer. "But the next day at work, I asked after her and the volunteer couldn't find her in our system. Later, I asked a different volunteer who couldn't find her either."

"That's odd."

"I know, right? Shannon said what probably happened was the pup's family came in before she was entered into the system and Paws just handed her over."

"That's not how it works," Cooper said, irritated at hearing the policies and practices weren't being followed. Policies he'd worked very hard to establish when he had first taken on the director role eight years earlier. He made a mental note to meet with Shannon first thing Monday morning—which was, like, the fourth thing he had to do "first thing" Monday—and to ensure she spoke to every intake desk volunteer on the matter.

"She said sometimes it's just easier." Annabeth pointed again to the computer screen. "That's Solstice. I'm sure of it."

"What? No. How?"

"I don't know, but I'm telling you that's my dog. See the white patch above her eye? It's in the shape of a parallelogram? A leaning rectangle. That's her. I know her face. I know her white patch. I'm telling you."

She said it with such conviction, with such certainty, how could he not believe it? He wished he could better remember what the dog she'd been petting looked like, but it was nowhere in his mind. He'd been looking at her that day. And every day since then.

"Let me get this straight. What you're telling me is a dog got put in our drop-off room one night. The next day there is no record of the dog in our system and a day or two later he ends up on Craigslist?"

"She. Solstice is a girl dog. Right, except for one thing."

"She, sorry. What one thing?"

"It wasn't a dog that got dropped off. It was a puppy."

"Right, okay. Whatever."

"No, not whatever. What did we just talk about at lunch?"

"No," he said automatically when he finally understood. "It can't be."

"It might not explain the guy with the gun, or give us any insight into what the heck he was looking for, but maybe it explains the decline in adoptions," she said.

"But to what end? Why?"

Annabeth got up and walked to the computer. She leaned over and read something on the screen. "How about a two hundred fifty dollar rehoming fee?"

Cooper's head was swimming. It was almost incomprehensible. He wasn't quite ready to make the leap that Annabeth had. "One dog does not a conspiracy make, even if that is the dog from drop-off."

Annabeth returned to her place on the couch next to him. "It is. Almost incomprehensible, I mean. And, I think you're wrong. But you're right…I can't prove it. Think about it, though. Every lead we've come up with has been a long shot. All so far outside the box that, by now, we've lost the box. This one—I don't know—this one feels right. I'm telling you. We're on to something. This lead is different. I think Solstice is just the tip of the iceberg."

"If you're right, you know what this means, don't you?" Cooper felt this like a stone in his stomach.

Neither said anything for a minute until Annabeth finally verbalized what he was thinking. She spoke evenly and slowly. "If this was not an isolated incident, if seeing Solstice for sale on Craigslist is the reason for the decline in puppy adoption fees at Paws, there is only one conclusion to be drawn." She paused. "It means someone at Paws is stealing dogs."

The stone in Cooper's stomach doubled in size when it was actually said out loud. "I have no idea how or why, but this is tied to Tuesday night. It's just too big of a coincidence not to be."

"I know," Annabeth agreed. "I have one more conclusion."

Cooper wasn't sure his stomach could take it.

"I don't see how it can be a volunteer. There isn't anyone at the office often enough or with enough consistency. I mean, several people could potentially be involved, but I really think it has to include—"

"An employee," Cooper finished for her. It made him ill. He'd personally hired every single employee now that Maggie was no longer there. Well, technically not Annabeth, since the board had hired her during his absence.

His mood was somber. Truth be told, he was a little heartbroken and, if this turned out to be true, betrayed. Cooper went through the employee roster and he just couldn't imagine a single one of them doing something like this.

For what was left of the afternoon, they went over it again and again, each time reaching the same conclusion. The pieces fit. They worked out the logistics of how the scheme likely worked. It wasn't complicated. They talked about each employee, trying to figure out who was the most likely candidate of such deception. On this matter, Annabeth contributed little. She was simply too new to know her co-workers on anything but a superficial level. But Cooper knew them and, each time, he dismissed the possibility that it could be any one of them.

Finally, they came up with a plan to ferret out the guilty party.

Not long after, there was a knock on the door.

Rusty didn't wait for them to answer before he walked in, followed by a swirl of cold air and Moose. He looked at the two of them, then looked at the kitchen table and said, "Where's my dinner? I thought it would be on the table by the time I got here."

"We got sidetracked," Cooper said and stood. "Lost track of time."

Rusty looked at the lines etched in his brother's face and said, "What's wrong?"

"Come on," Cooper motioned with his head for Rusty to follow him into the kitchen. "It'll only take a few minutes to have dinner ready. We'll microwave the leftovers." Rusty followed while Moose demanded pets from Annabeth, who remained on the couch. "We'll fill you in over dinner. Then you need to do something for us."

~ * ~

"Ready?" Rusty asked.

Cooper and Annabeth nodded. Rusty hit the final button on his phone. It was on speaker so they all listened as it rang.

On the fourth ring, a man answered. "Hello?"

"Hi," Rusty said. "I saw your listing on Craigslist. About the dog."

"Which one?"

"What?" Rusty asked confused.

"I'm moving to another country and have three dogs. I'm trying to find good homes for all of them. Which one were you interested in?"

Cooper saw that Annabeth had gone pale. She clasped her hand over her mouth as if to stifle a scream. Both men looked at her.

She moved her hand and mouthed, "That's him." Then made a gun with her finger.

"You sure?" Cooper whispered.

"That's him," she mouthed again.

"Hey, buddy?" they all heard through the speaker.

"Yeah, I'm here," Rusty said. "You cut out for a minute. I'm interested in the black Lab."

~ * ~

Cooper handed Annabeth her glass of port. This was becoming a thing, he thought, amused. Night number three. He kind of liked it and would miss it when this was over. And that could be very soon. Maybe even tomorrow. A nightcap alone just wouldn't be the same.

As if reading his mind, Annabeth said, "I can't believe we did it. We figured this out."

"Let's not get ahead of ourselves. We have a long way to go. We still don't know who is involved. And, maybe more importantly, we don't why the tall man was after you."

"All true, but I'm choosing to celebrate tonight. Cheers," she said, even though both had already taken sips from their glasses.

He clinked her glass. "Cheers."

"If everything goes perfectly, we might be able to put all this stress and chaos and people shooting at us—at you—behind us. I've been in this zombie-like zone for the past four days. It's almost going to feel weird to go back to normal. To be able to sleep in my own bed. To not worry what I'll find when I open my office door."

To not constantly be worried about you, Cooper thought. "It will be weird. Who will I have a nip with after this?"

Annabeth smiled. "You'll find someone."

He wanted to tell her that he thought he already had, but he knew how she felt.

"Have you thought anymore about who might be behind this?" she asked.

"Haven't been able to stop thinking about it. I still cannot imagine it's anyone at Paws, but I know it must be."

"If you had to make a guess, who would you say?" Annabeth asked. "I mean, it has to be someone."

He didn't want to guess. Mostly because he didn't want it to be true. "I don't know," he said for the dozenth time. "But if I absolutely had to say—"

"You do."

"I'd say Simon. He's been asking me to increase his hours from thirty-two to forty for the last few years because it's hard financially not to be working forty hours. And money's the motive, right? As facility manager, he has keys to absolutely everything. Not that it matters. But he can, and does, go everywhere without anyone questioning it. But I'm sure it's not him."

"You're sure it's not anyone," she said gently.

"I know."

"Hey," she said suddenly. "Why didn't I think of this before?" She jumped up and went back to the computer and started clicking on the keyboard. He followed and stood behind her as she got first into the financial files, then into the payroll files.

As she clicked through various screens, she said, "Now there is no way to know if the person started this scheme immediately after getting hired, or if the person had been around for years before coming up with the idea." A few more screens went by. "But—" She pointed to the screen. "Look. Only one person started three years ago."

Twenty-two

If Annabeth thought the night before had been her worst night's sleep since this whole thing started, she was in for a rude awakening. Her mind simply would not quiet. Over and over again, she mentally scripted the scene where the appointment to meet the black Lab ended with the gunman and his accomplice, whoever it turned out to be, in prison. But considering the man had a gun and he wasn't afraid to use it, Annabeth played out every possible way things could go wrong. It was futile, but she attempted to script a counterplan for every possibility. One after another. Until her phone told her it was morning.

To make matters worse, she and Cooper had dragged Rusty into the mess. Cooper said Rusty was fine, but Annabeth still felt bad. Still, they had no choice. The gunman had seen both Annabeth and Cooper.

Even without sleep, morning came as a relief. Maybe getting up and moving could help her find a way out of her own head. Images of the worst-case scenarios were worse than nightmares. They paralyzed her with fear. By the early morning, doubts about their plans had started to seep in.

After her morning shower, she went into the kitchen. Cooper looked as rough around the edges as she felt. Tired eyes and a general droopiness. "You look like you slept about as well as I did," she said.

"It's going to be a two-pot day," he said, taking the carafe from the coffee maker and filling a mug for her.

"Indeed," she said and plopped down at the kitchen table. Cooper's in-box remained on one of the chairs, and it didn't seem likely the foot-high stack would be getting smaller any time soon.

They drank that first cup of coffee in silence, each fighting fatigue and the battles in their own minds. Annabeth knew Cooper was particularly upset that one of his own employees could betray the company to such an unforgivable extent. He took it as a personal affront to his ability as a leader, as the one in charge.

When Cooper got up to refill their mugs, he added four slices of bread to the toaster.

"I'm so tired but can't sleep. It feels like my body is trying to escape its own skin," Annabeth said.

"Me, too. The appointment is four hours from now. What should we do until then? Afterward, I expect to sleep for a week."

They went through a string of ideas, but nothing sparked. Work? No. Play a game? No. Besides, he didn't have any. Go for a walk? No, took too much energy. Sleep? They both laughed at that one.

"Drink?" Annabeth offered.

"Ha. Now that's the best idea yet. But, no, we have to be alert and clear."

"Not to mention it's eight o'clock on a Sunday morning," Annabeth added.

He didn't have television and didn't subscribe to any of the streaming services, so mindless entertainment was out. Although Annabeth thought a heavy action, heavy drama might be perfect. It would build their confidence since, in movies, right is always victorious after several defeats and tests. This past week they certainly had been tested. More than she ever could've imagined possible seven weeks ago when she had walked into Rescued Paws to begin a new chapter of her life. How could anyone imagine a week like the one they'd had? It was not possible.

The minutes dripped by like sap down forest trees. Slow. Painfully slow. In the end, they continued to sit at the kitchen table drinking coffee. One or the other occasionally tossed out an idea of something to do to make the time move faster but, ultimately, every idea was rejected.

Until...

The stakeout was Cooper's idea.

"If we are going to sit around staring into thin air, why don't we make use of all that staring? At least I'd feel like I was doing something instead of nothing."

"What are you talking about?" Annabeth asked.

"It might be for nothing. In fact, I'm sure it'll be for nothing. But what if we went to the tall man's house, or the appointment address if it isn't his house, and stare at that for a while? Who knows? Maybe we'll see something."

Annabeth wasn't exactly sure what he thought they might see, but she agreed, because anything had to be better than sitting at Cooper's table doing nothing.

It took them about an hour before they were ready to leave the cabin. They piled blankets into the truck along with a thermos of very hot tomato soup and a small paper sack filled with saltine crackers.

They stopped at Rusty's cabin to tell him about their plan, which Rusty promptly tried to talk them out of. He thought a stakeout was a terrible idea, that they risked being seen and blowing everything. But Cooper couldn't be dissuaded. He promised his brother they'd be careful.

Annabeth added, "This way we can be your backup. We'll watch as you go look at the dog."

"I don't need backup."

"We just can't sit around and do nothing," Cooper said. "We'll stay several houses away. No one will see us. Don't worry. You remember the plan?"

"Brother, it's not complicated. I go in. I see the dog. I ask to see the other dogs. I take photos of them all. I say I have to talk to my wife about it. And I leave."

"In and out," Cooper said.

"In and out," Rusty repeated.

"That man is a bad dude," Cooper said as if his brother didn't already know.

Rusty made one more attempt to get them not to head into town, but Cooper was determined and Annabeth followed his lead.

They said goodbye and Annabeth and Cooper were on their way to Anchorage. Annabeth didn't want to admit it out loud because it was a grave situation, she knew that, but it was kind of thrilling, too. Her first ever stakeout. Hopefully her last. But still...

They easily found the address. It wasn't the same address as the one they had on file for the employee who had started three years earlier. But that didn't mean anything, one way or the other. It was a small older house on a block with other small older houses.

To kill a little more time, they drove the neighborhood, blasting the heater on high to fill the cab with as much hot air as possible. An alley ran behind the house. But they agreed it would be risky to drive down and being seen wasn't a risk they could take, though both really wanted to see the back side of the house.

Cooper pulled into a parking spot behind a large black SUV three houses down on the opposite side of the street. They felt confident that, should anyone look out a window, they wouldn't spot two people sitting in a truck down the block.

They secured blankets over their legs. Cooper handed Annabeth a small pair of binoculars. "I only had one pair at the cabin so we'll have to share."

Because of the SUV, Annabeth being in the passenger's side meant she didn't have a full view of the house, but she could see everything from the front door over. "You would know better than I," she said. "But I don't recognize any of the vehicles out front. Do you?"

Cooper put his hand out for the binoculars and looked through them. "I didn't think to look. But no, I'm not seeing any employee's car."

"Could be in the back," Annabeth said.

"Or in that single car garage next to the house," Cooper said, from under the binoculars.

The garage was out of Annabeth's line of sight, but she had seen it when they drove by. Annabeth laughed and Cooper lowered the binoculars to look at her. "I have no idea why I just thought of this. But I heard on one of those morning radio trivia segments that something like seventy-five percent of Alaskans with garages don't actually use them for their cars. That's crazy. Why would you choose to start a car in the cold dark winter months if you didn't have to? The first minutes are downright painful as I wait for mine to get warm enough to drive to work."

"Toys," he said. "Snow machines, four-wheelers and just plain junk. I bet people wish they could park in their garages, but simply don't have the room."

"That's crazy," Annabeth repeated. "Do you park in your garage at home?"

"I wish. I don't actually have a garage. But I do have a huge lot, so building one has been on my to-do list since I bought the place."

"When did you buy it?"

He laughed. "I don't want to say."

"Now you have to."

"Six years ago."

Annabeth tried to not laugh, but it proved impossible. Maybe it was deliriousness from lack of sleep, but to have something on the to-do list for six years struck her as funny.

They settled in and did the exact same thing they'd done at Cooper's cabin. Sat and stared. But somehow, the time wasn't dripping by like it had been before. It might be very little, but little as it was, it felt like they were doing something. Only ninety minutes until the appointment.

Annabeth looked over at Cooper, who stared ahead, his eyes half closed and his head fighting gravity. She had to admit, she was going to miss this. Not the fear, obviously. Or someone being after them.

But the intrigue, working closely with Cooper toward a common goal. Normal life was going to be dull by comparison.

The interior of the truck got colder and colder. The heat they'd captured before parking was long gone. "Maybe we should have that soup now," Annabeth said, not wanting to suggest turning the truck on, though that's what she desperately wanted.

Neither remembered to bring something for them to eat from or with, and Cooper had left his emergency food duffel in the cabin to replace what they'd eaten at Mrs. B's B&B. They only had the top of the thermos to use. So, they took turns. First Annabeth sipped a cup full. Then Cooper. Then Annabeth. Then Cooper. It was a relatively small cup. She didn't care. The soup was still hot and helped warm her insides.

It warmed her enough she thought she could go another little while without heat. While Cooper enjoyed his turn sipping the hot soup, she tucked the blanket tighter around her legs.

When they were down to the last half hour, Cooper, Annabeth was pretty sure, dozed off. It was hard to tell between that and sitting with his head back and his eyes closed. But the deep slow breaths made her think he was more than just resting his eyes. She still felt exhausted and wide awake at the same time.

Annabeth stared at the house, wondering what was going on behind that front door, hoping the dogs were not being mistreated.

Then as if her own thoughts made it happen, the front door opened. Her eyes widened. It was so unexpected.

Annabeth sucked in her breath when a black puppy emerged on a leash. Her black puppy. The dog was followed by the gunman who stayed in the frame of the door. Stunned, Annabeth couldn't move. She couldn't even breathe.

The pup sniffed, peed, sniffed some more. The gunman, who wasn't wearing a coat, said something and yanked on the leash, causing Solstice to trip in the snow.

"No," Annabeth said loudly. Then, without a single thought in her head, she opened the truck door and started running down the sidewalk.

She hadn't gotten further than the distance of one house when she face-planted in the soft pile of snow in someone's yard. Cooper had tackled her.

He'd fallen next to her, so she turned over on her back to face him. "Why'd you do that?" she said angrily. But she knew.

"Do you want to ruin everything?" he said right back. "What were you thinking?"

"I wasn't. I don't know. I just reacted. Did you see? The dog?"

"I didn't see anything except you running," he admitted. Cooper, who had landed on his stomach, rose on his hands and peered between two vehicles to see the house. "There's nothing there now."

"The tall man brought Solstice out the front door to pee," Annabeth explained. "I'm sorry. I'm almost never impulsive, but I wasn't thinking. He pulled on the leash and made her fall. I just wanted to save my dog." She bit her tongue to try to keep from crying, but the thought of Solstice with the gunman was too much. Tears slid down the sides of her face and pooled in her ears. The cold froze the tears to her eyelashes.

"You okay now?"

She wasn't but indicated she was with a nod.

"No more running?"

"No."

"We stick to the plan. And if everything goes south, we'll send Rusty back to buy Solstice, okay? I promise. Now let's get back to the truck before anyone sees us. Or before we get hypothermia."

Annabeth knew he had no business making that promise. Still, she adored him for doing so. She loved the confidence with which he said it. And she so desperately wanted to believe they would rescue Solstice.

The minute or so they'd been lying in the snow, Annabeth regained her wits. She decided she wasn't going to do anything stupid when it came to the dog.

But she decided something else, too. Different and, perhaps, equally stupid. When Cooper rose up on his hands again from his position on his stomach to make sure it was safe for them to make their way back to the truck, Annabeth grabbed the front of his jacket with both hands and pulled him toward her.

His lips met hers. Soft, at first, and though both had cold faces, in a matter of seconds, Annabeth felt warmth from his lips and then his tongue. She urgently pulled him down to her, closer, kissed him harder. Warmth radiated down her body. She tingled at her core.

Annabeth pushed his chest away. He looked down on her, his breath shallow, their noses only inches apart. "Now that's a memorable first kiss," Annabeth said. She raised her head and met his lips softly again, then pushed him aside, got up and walked back to the truck.

Cooper caught up to her, his breath still ragged. He helped brush the snow clinging to her backside and she did the same for him, though most of his snow was on his front. They didn't speak. They stomped hard to get snow off their feet. And when most of it was off, Cooper opened the passenger door and waited for Annabeth to crawl back into the passenger seat before closing her door. Then he walked around the truck and got in on his side.

No amount of tomato soup and blankets could get them warm now as they were wet in places where snow clung to their clothes. Cooper turned on the truck, though quickly turned off the headlights which had gone on automatically. He left the heater off and Annabeth knew after the time they'd sat there, it would only blow out cold air. It was going to take a few minutes for the engine to warm.

"You were right about one thing," Cooper finally spoke. "That was an amazing first—well, second—kiss." Annabeth looked over to see a silly grin spread over his face.

She smiled. She couldn't help it. Then she shook her head. "I need to be clear about one thing. That will not happen again. It was a one-time thing you didn't do properly the first time. I was merely righting a wrong."

He laughed.

She did, too. But she was serious. She hated saying it. Hated that it was true. But it could not happen again. She had finished what he had started by kissing her in the Whittier underground corridor.

"You sure?" he asked.

"Yes. It's out of my system now." She thought it worth repeating to make sure he knew she was firm in her decision. "Because we don't know how it's going to work out," she said pointing to the house. "I wanted one thing to be good. That's why I did it. One sure thing. But I already told you, I refuse to be that person again. The one who has an affair with her boss."

"Would it be an affair if neither of us is married? Technically speaking." he asked.

"Yes, it absolutely would. Call it what you like, but I'm not doing it." *No matter how much I might want to*, she thought.

Before he could reply, Rusty's truck drove slowly by. Moose sat in the passenger seat, concentrating on the road ahead as if he were the one driving. It didn't matter, because what more was there to say?

"Here we go," Cooper said. He turned the heater on low. It was barely warm, but it wouldn't be long before it turned hot and they could turn it to high and get warmed through and through.

"He's parking in the driveway, in front of the garage," Cooper narrated since her view was blocked. Rusty got out and walked to the front door. It was opened by the tall lanky man. Rusty stepped in and the door shut.

The air in the truck, though warmer, was tense as they waited for Rusty to emerge. Ten slow minutes later, the front door opened and Rusty exited. Both Annabeth and Cooper let out an audible breath. Both, it seemed, had been holding theirs.

Rusty got in his truck and started it up. But he didn't move.

"What's he doing?" Annabeth asked.

"Can't see," Cooper said and put the binoculars up to his eyes. "There, he just fastened his seatbelt and pulled out of the driveway. He's driving the opposite way." A second later, Cooper's phone dinged. Cooper took off his gloves and dug the phone from his coat pocket. He punched in his security code, then looked at the phone.

He handed it to Annabeth and put the truck in reverse. Then pulled out from behind the SUV.

Annabeth looked at the screen. Three photos of three different puppies, including a black one with a white parallelogram above her right eye. Rusty's text instructed them to meet him in the parking lot of a grocery store a few blocks away.

Cooper pulled his truck alongside his brother's so Annabeth was closest to him. Rusty rolled his window down and Annabeth did the same.

Cooper leaned over toward Annabeth to hear Rusty better. "How did it go? Did he suspect anything?" Cooper asked.

"No. It was fine. The guy said a few other people looked at the dogs yesterday so I better let him know asap if I wanted one. First come, first serve, and he won't hold them."

"How did the dogs look?" Annabeth asked. "Did it seem like they were being mistreated?"

Rusty shook his head. "I don't know. Hard to say. But they seemed okay. They didn't act afraid of the guy or anything."

It was such a relief to hear. Annabeth bit her lip, afraid her voice might crack if she spoke.

"Did you see anyone else?" Cooper asked. Poor Cooper, Annabeth thought, still holding out hope that a Paws' employee wasn't involved.

"No, but I heard someone in a back room. Whoever it was never came out. I wasn't sure what all I should ask. We should've thought of new-owner questions last night so I sounded more interested. So, I asked the gender and how old they were. The only other thing I could think was to ask if they were healthy. The guy said he had taken them to the vet just a few weeks ago for vaccines. So, then I asked if I'd be able to get a copy of the records. I don't know. I thought maybe you could use them somehow."

"Good thinking," Cooper said. "What did he say?"

"He said it wasn't a problem. Said the vet was backed up because several of his staff were on vacation, but all the dogs would come with a health certificate. But said he might have to send it afterwards when the vet got it to him."

Annabeth whipped her head around to see if Cooper had heard the same thing she had. They both gave the other wide eyes.

"What?" Rusty asked. "What happened?"

"Bro, I think you just broke this case," Cooper said.

"What'd I say?"

"We have to go to the office. We'll meet you back at the cabin. Why don't you pick up a celebratory pizza for us? Maybe two. Hell, maybe three." Cooper was almost gleeful.

"Whatever," Rusty said. "Be careful. Call me if you need anything."

"Will do. Thanks, bro. You're my favorite brother."

Rusty rolled his eyes at Annabeth, closed his window and pulled away.

"You were right," Cooper admitted as he drove toward Rescued Paws.

"You don't know me very well," Annabeth teased him. "But you'll find I often am." She couldn't hide the huge smile on her face.

They talked as Cooper drove. Puzzle piece after puzzle piece fell into place until the full picture emerged. They agreed there was just one thing to double check at the office to confirm what they already knew. Then they'd drive directly to the police station, though neither had any idea if Detective Jones would be in. This couldn't wait until their appointment the next day.

In Cooper's office, he shed his coat and dumped it on the floor. Annabeth took a chair while he looked for the blue binder. She offered to help, but she knew how it was. It's easier to find something in your own mess than to direct someone else to help. Besides, she just wanted to sit and watch him in his glee. For the first time since everything started, the tension in his face was gone. No doubt, the same was true for her.

Annabeth felt herself smiling big. It was finally over. They had figured it out. They'd no longer be in danger. The bad guys really would be behind bars.

Her glee dissolved right out of her when she heard the distinct sound of the front door of Paws unlock and then open. "Did you hear that?" she whispered.

"Yes," Cooper said. "Hide. I'll go check it out."

What? There was no way she was letting him go alone. "Maybe it was nothing. I'm going with you. We're in this together, right?"

"At least stay behind me. Just in case," Cooper said. He frantically looked around, then grabbed a metal letter opener from the pencil cup on his desk.

Annabeth helped herself to a pair of scissors. Cooper started to say something but then thought better of it.

"Behind me," he said again, more firmly this time. "I will not let anything happen to you." And she believed him.

They followed the corridor down to the front lobby. Annabeth experienced that odd sensation called *déjà vu*. This was exactly where everything had started five nights earlier.

They rounded the corner. What they saw did not surprise Annabeth. But, still, somehow, she found it shocking. There he was again. The tall man. And, like before, he held a gun pointed directly at her and Cooper.

But unlike five nights ago, this time he was not alone.

Twenty-three

Cooper couldn't deny it any longer. He'd so hoped they'd been wrong. Somehow, he desperately hoped it wasn't an employee. But now, face-to-face with her, his denial obliterated.

"Shannon," he said.

"Cooper," she said.

"Why?" Cooper said.

Shannon didn't reply.

Annabeth answered. "Because she could. Because she didn't think she'd get caught. Because she cared more about easy money than about being a decent human being."

That got Shannon's attention. "I am a good person. I made sure every one of the dogs went to a good home."

"How did you justify stealing from Paws? From me?" Cooper wanted to know.

"Enough with the chit-chat," Shannon's tall companion said. "Let's get what we came here for. Do what we need to do and get out."

"Do what you need to do?" Cooper heard Annabeth repeat in a whisper.

Surely a few thousand dollars wasn't worth killing two people, Cooper thought. That cannot be what he meant. Keep them talking.

Stall as long as possible and look for an opening. Cooper reached his hand around to his back pocket to make sure the letter opener was still where he had put it before they rounded the corner. He hoped Annabeth had done something equally strategic with the scissors she'd grabbed from his desk.

"How did it start?" Cooper asked Shannon.

"I said enough with the chit-chat," the tall man said loudly, pointing the gun to the center of Cooper's chest.

"You want the adoption certificates? Then you'll tell me." Cooper ignored the man and kept his eyes on Shannon's.

"We don't care about the adoption certificates," Shannon said.

"I know. You want the health certificates that are attached to the adoption certificates to give to the people buying the dogs you stole. That's what your thug was looking for that first night. What? Couldn't find a vet to pull into your scheme?"

"Who you calling a thug?" the man shook the gun in Cooper's direction and Cooper heard Annabeth suck in her breath. Instinctively, he stuck his arm out to shield her.

"Jake. Calm down. He's just trying to distract you. Focus," Shannon counseled. He didn't move. "Honey?" she said softer, touching his arm. He looked at her. She spoke to him using just her eyes and the man—Jake—lowered the gun slightly.

"The certificates. Now," Jake said.

Cooper turned his attention to Shannon, though he kept one eye on the gun. "You didn't answer my question."

"It's not an exciting story," Shannon said. "It just happened. One day after I first started here, I was printing out all the adoption and health certificates, and the idea just came to me. You signed the whole stack. Then Maggie prepared them for mailing. Nobody ever actually looks at them. Even if you did, you wouldn't know one dog from another. I only meant to do a few. Pay off my car. But then, when no one noticed—" she trailed off.

"When the certificates ended up back at your office, you pulled out the ones from the dogs you stole," Cooper said, finishing the story of how she had pulled it off.

"It was almost too easy," Shannon said proudly, which sickened Cooper. How could he have been so wrong about her? "We made a lot of money."

"Money." Annabeth said. Cooper turned to look at her. "I just remembered something." She looked at Cooper. "I couldn't remember anything the thug had said that night except 'money' but now it just came back to me. All of a sudden. He kept saying that no one was coming between him and his money. Why couldn't I remember that earlier?"

"It's okay," Cooper said. "It wouldn't have made a difference."

"There. I told you. Let's get the certificates," Shannon said.

"Why do you need them now?" Annabeth asked. "You're caught. It's over."

"It might be over, but we aren't caught. We have the gun. We'll finally get these damned certificates, deliver another fifteen dogs tonight. Collect the money and then we're out of here. After I paid off the car, it's a good thing I kept most of what we made over the last three years. It'll last us a long time where we're going."

"Where are you going?" Annabeth asked.

Shannon looked at her like she was the dirty gum stuck to the bottom of her shoe. "Shut up. You stupid—"

"Focus," Jake said to her.

"Certificates. Now," Shannon demanded. "Then Jake here is going to tie you up good and tight. We'll be long gone by the time anyone finds you tomorrow."

Cooper didn't know how much longer he could stall so he said, "In my office."

"How'd you know we were here?" Annabeth asked.

"Because you two are idiots," Jake said, waggling the gun to get them to move. Cooper and Annabeth partially turned in the direction of the hall that would lead them to the T that would lead to Cooper's office. He didn't dare take his eyes off of them completely.

"You think I wouldn't recognize another Cooper?" Shannon asked. "You two could be twins. Then I look outside and what do I see? The two of you. Sitting outside my house. Do you think I'm stupid?"

Cooper stopped and turned to face Shannon directly. "Yeah, I kind of do," he said. He turned back again to give Annabeth a look but the look she returned said she had no idea what he was doing.

"What?" Shannon said, high-pitched in surprise and anger.

Cooper continued to look at Annabeth, keeping Shannon in his peripheral vision. He laughed. Then Cooper said to Annabeth, "Never underestimate the stupidity of criminals. Isn't that an expression? These geniuses here would've continued to get away with it if they'd just held tight."

"What? What do you mean?" Shannon demanded.

Cooper ignored her, continued to speak to Annabeth. "But they panicked, not knowing when I would come back from my leave. The certificates piled up. My first day back—though, of course, no one knew I was back—and they come looking for them. Talk about terrible timing."

Cooper laughed harder, confusing everyone. "You know the funny thing?"

"No," Annabeth said, trying to play her part even if she didn't really understand her part.

"You know that night Jake here had the gun pointed at you, and I came around the corner?"

"Yes," Annabeth said.

Cooper caught a look between Shannon and Jake. "Remember I hit him?" Cooper laughed even harder.

"I remember."

"The blue binder I hit him with was filled with two months' worth of certificates I'd just finished signing."

Annabeth tried to laugh, too.

"Literally. Just. Finished. Signing." Cooper turned to Shannon. "I was bringing them to your office. So, you see if you'd just waited one more day, just twelve more hours, no one would've been the wiser."

Shannon was red in the face with anger. "I should have him shoot you," she spat out. "Now move."

"Oh," Jake said eerily calmly. "I am going to shoot him. Both of them."

"What? No," Shannon said.

"Yep," Jake said. "We're not tying them up. We're going for a more permanent solution."

Shannon tried not to show shock on her face, but she failed. Clearly, they had different ideas about what was going to happen next. Cooper hoped to capitalize on the moment. At some point, he was going to have to try to get that gun away from Jake. Again. And he was running out of time.

"Jake, no. That's not what we agreed," she said. Cooper could hear tension—fear—in her voice. She might have a stomach for theft and fraud, but she was no killer. "Honey, we just need enough time to get out of town."

"And if they can't talk, we'll have a bigger head start."

"Either way," Shannon tried to reason with him. "Someone will find them tomorrow when Paws opens."

"Not if we dump their bodies. We could have several days before anyone is the wiser."

Shannon grabbed Jake's arm to plead with him and Cooper thought it was now or never. It was unlikely he'd get a better opportunity.

Jake looked at Shannon and that's when Cooper sprang. He wanted to tackle his whole body but needed to concentrate on the gun. So, he dove for Jake's arm. With both hands, he grabbed Jake's arm to swing the gun away.

Like in a tunnel, Shannon's scream sounded distant and hollow to Cooper.

Then the gun exploded, searing Cooper's left hand wrapped around the barrel, though he hardly felt it. Another scream. This time it was Annabeth and he knew by the sound, she'd been hit. Hers was a scream of agony.

The men fell to the ground with a thud. Jake took the brunt of the blow on his back with Cooper landing on top of him. As Jake tried to recover his breath, Cooper reached behind and pulled the letter opener from his back pocket. He didn't aim. He just stabbed.

Jake let out a blood-curdling scream of pain, drowning out any sound either woman was making. He scrambled away from

Cooper, leaving a blood trail from his leg, the hilt of the letter opener protruding from the side of his thigh. The gun dropped, forgotten in the tall man's effort to get away. With his good leg, he kicked at Cooper. He made contact with the same side of his face he had five nights earlier. Cooper's head whipped to the side and he fell hard on the floor, smacking the opposite side of his head.

Immediately the room started to spin and go fuzzy. Cooper didn't think he could move. His head throbbed and a black ring started closing in. Somewhere in his mind he heard footsteps and the door open, just like that first night. He might have heard a car. Cooper heard grunting beside him. Jake was coming back at him. Cooper couldn't move. Then a blur passed by him. He heard more grunting and then quiet. Cooper was confused. He didn't know what had just happened. But one last time he looked over at Jake to see the handle of a pair of scissors stuck in his chest.

At least, he thought, Annabeth is alive. She is safe now.

Then everything went black.

Twenty-four

Annabeth's skin was itchy Not just under the cast on her arm, but her whole body. She was on pins and needles, crawling out of her skin and every other cliché she could think of. It was almost Christmas, 12 days since she'd been shot in the arm, shattering her radius bone. Over the last almost two weeks, she'd had multiple surgeries, a blood clot complication and a whole lot of pain.

She teased her surgeon that she expected to have a bionic arm after all the hardware he'd put in. Luckily, she spent most of those days on very heavy pain management medications dripped in through the IV in her good arm.

Her surgeon had visited two hours earlier and finally issued her walking orders. She'd pled with him for the last three days to be released. It was such a relief to know she'd be going home. He said he'd write her a couple of prescriptions and advised her to stay ahead of the pain. In other words, take the pills whether she thought she needed them or not because it wasn't worth the risk of letting the drug get out of her system. In another 10 days, she'd move to the less strong pills and then she'd move to over-the-counter pain relief. He told her the nurse would go over her discharge instructions, as well as information for the physical therapy she'd need once the cast was removed.

"Who knew getting shot in the arm could be so complicated?" Annabeth said, not for the first time.

"You got shot in the worst possible place, at the worst possible angle. If it had been any worse, we might have had to amputate," he said, also not for the first time. Now that she was past the critical part, they could joke. But Annabeth had overheard two nurses talking after the first surgery when they thought she was asleep. In short, they verified that she really had almost lost the arm. She was lucky.

A bit ago, as promised, the nurse had come in with those instructions. Then he removed her from the monitors and took out the IV. Now as she sat in the chair waiting for the last of the paperwork, her head a little clearer, she could reflect on the past two weeks. Two totally insane never-hope-to-repeat weeks.

She'd been pleased, and a little surprised, by the number of visitors during her days in the hospital. Three of her former co-workers from Gibson & Gellar stopped by on their lunch hour on day three. They'd brought a lovely pink flower arrangement from the entire office. The vase would be going home with her, but the wilting and dying flowers were in the garbage can in the bathroom.

A few days ago, Gil Gibson came. He brought a box of her favorite marzipan and dark chocolate candies. They had a nice chat and, in the end, he helped Annabeth figure a few things out. She'd forever be grateful for knowing him and for having him as a person in her corner.

Zoey came by on behalf of the staff and volunteers at Paws and brought her a lovely silk scarf. The card said she could wear it when she returned to work. Annabeth was grateful Zoey hadn't asked for details or brought up Shannon. The flowers from the board of directors arrived on her second day in the hospital.

The visit from Maggie yesterday morning had surprised her the most. Like Zoey, she didn't stay long, but brought Annabeth a big Get Well Soon balloon and two jars of her jam. The same jam Annabeth had tasted at Cooper's cabin.

Maggie told her not to worry about things at Paws, because Cooper had asked her to help out until after the New Year when he hoped she, Annabeth, would be back on her feet. Annabeth smiled when Maggie told her that all the staff got the same two jars of jam she'd just received as an early Christmas gift. She smiled even bigger knowing how happy Maggie's jam allotment would make Cooper.

Visitor might not be the right word to describe the first person waiting for her when she woke from her initial surgery. During that first visit, Detective Mitchell Jones was allowed to spend only a few minutes questioning her because she was so groggy. So groggy, in fact, she didn't even remember talking to him even after he told her about it during his second visit. He assured her that she had been quite helpful and the heavy medication hadn't caused her to say anything embarrassing. Well, not too embarrassing because, apparently, she did tell Detective Jones several times how sweet he was. "Like candy," he reported were her words. Jones' second visit came two days after the first. He stayed for several hours to fill in all the details of the events.

Despite what she thought at the time, it turned out Annabeth had not killed Jake. When she stabbed him in the chest, the shears went between two ribs and collapsed one of his lungs. He'd been in the hospital—both hands cuffed to the bed, the detective assured her—until that morning when he was sent to the medical unit at the jail. A place he wouldn't be leaving anytime soon.

The night of the confrontation, Annabeth had called 911, and help (both police and paramedics) arrived in less than five minutes. Despite excruciating pain, she was able to provide the police with enough information that they sent someone immediately to Shannon's house where they found her frantically packing.

Both Shannon and Jake couldn't talk fast enough, each wanting to testify against the other in hopes of getting a better deal. But all that was for the prosecutor's office to sort out. Detective Jones felt confident they'd both take a plea deal, ensuring neither Annabeth nor Cooper would have to testify in court. It turned out Shannon had removed Annabeth's keys from her office the day after the initial encounter with Jake. She'd gone to the hardware store a few blocks down and had a copy made. That's why there'd been no sign of a break-in at her apartment. And, of course, he'd simply used Shannon's key to get into the building that first night.

But Annabeth's biggest surprise wasn't a visitor at all. In fact, it was the opposite. The biggest surprise was a non-visitor. Not once during her 12 days in the hospital had Cooper come by to see her.

It stung, she had to admit. After all they'd been through.

She learned from Detective Jones that Cooper had stayed in the hospital for three days. Jake had broken Cooper's nose, which explained all the blood when Annabeth got to him after he'd blacked out. But, unlike the first time he hit his head, this time the professionals insisted he stay for observation. Not that he could tell them no, being unconscious and all. Two bad head bangs, including one where he lost consciousness, were nothing to mess around with. He'd gotten the all-clear the same day as Detective Jones' second visit. Annabeth had been so relieved to hear he'd be okay.

Finally, the nurse returned with a clipboard. Annabeth signed several documents, listened one last time to her discharge instructions, took two written prescriptions and stuffed them into her coat pocket. She asked the nurse to give her Get Well Soon balloon to a patient who could use cheering up. Then she asked him to call her a cab.

Annabeth looked around the sterile room to make sure she had everything. Before she left, she called the front desk of Rescued Paws. The volunteer was confused by what Annabeth asked of him. But after a second explanation, he transferred Annabeth directly through to Cooper's voice mail. Annabeth left a message to let him know she had been discharged and would be at Paws in two hours and that she needed to talk to him. It was important, she emphasized.

When she pulled into the parking lot at Rescued Paws, Annabeth felt like a new woman. The shower had done wonders for her, even if it took twice as long as normal with her arm in a garbage bag, poking outside the shower curtain. With one hand, the shampoo bottle alone took a full minute to open. It had been startling to arrive at her apartment to find it in disarray from the night of the break-in. She'd given Detective Jones her keys to get into her apartment for the photos the police needed and she saw the telltale sign of black fingerprint dust in a few places. But she would have plenty of time to get things orderly again.

Her stomach knotted. Why was she so nervous? She knew why. The conversation she planned to have with Cooper. It wasn't going to be an easy one. She'd been practicing it in her head for days, ever since Gil's visit. She wasn't sure how to tell Cooper. But it had to be done.

On top of the nervous stomach, her arm started to throb, radiating pain through her entire body. Out of the hospital two hours and she was already defying doctor's orders. But she needed to get this conversation behind her and she knew she wouldn't be able to drive if she took a pain pill. It said so right on the label.

She'd hoped to sneak in and go right to Cooper's office. But no such luck. Everyone came to greet her in the lobby, to ask how she was doing, to express their gratitude for what she had done for Paws and the dogs. Annabeth spent a few minutes with her co-workers, making sure they knew how much she appreciated the scarf and how she looked forward to wearing it very soon. She excused herself and went to Cooper's office.

She knocked lightly on his door then opened it.

Cooper sat behind his desk, head down. Deep in paperwork. He looked up and a big grin spread across his horrible looking, yet still very handsome, face.

"Ouch," he said, touching the side of his face. "Smiling hurts. Frowning hurts. Everything hurts," he laughed.

Though almost two weeks had passed, the entire side of his face was bruised blue, plus both eyes were racoon black. He had many more weeks before his face would be back to normal. Kind of like her arm. He came around his desk and gave her a light, very gentle hug.

"How are you?" he said, pointing to the cast.

"In need of a pain pill," she answered honestly. "It took pins and plates and screws and I don't know what else to put my arm back together. There might actually be some superglue and duct tape in there somewhere. But I'm going to be fine. Back to normal in a few months."

"We're practically twins." He lifted his left hand. Annabeth saw the white bandage wrapped around the entire thing from fingertips to wrist, his lone thumb left unwrapped. She'd forgotten about that.

Not about the gunshot, obviously, but about Cooper grabbing the gun and the smell of burning flesh. When Annabeth got to him after she'd stabbed Jake, she's been so concerned for his face, his bloody nose and the fact that he was unconscious that she never even looked at the damage to his hand.

"At least it was our left arms," Annabeth said.

"I'm so glad you came by," he said sweetly, a sentiment she was about to rip into. "I have to apologize to you. I meant to come by the hospital," he started.

She cut him off. "No, please don't. You are a hero in all this. You don't owe me an apology or an explanation."

"Well, as I was saying, I meant to come by the hospital when you were awake. I did visit. I came by twice while I was in the hospital, two floors above you. But you were sleeping both times. Then I came by once after I got out, but it was the day they took you back into surgery. Things have been crazy. Between the police and here. I meant to get back again, but—"

"Entirely understandable. I'm sure you've been overwhelmed. Don't worry," she said.

"Hey, guess what Maggie told me? Three more people got locked in the underground corridor in Whittier the same week we did. Turns out two kids dared another kid to do it. The kid was a maintenance worker's grandson, which is how he got his grubby little hands on the keys. We were the first, but not the last."

"She told me when I saw her at the hospital," Annabeth said.

"Did she tell you I asked her to fill in until you're ready to come back?" he asked.

"Can we sit?" she asked. They took their usual seats at his little meeting table. "First, I want to say thanks. For everything. I mean it. You are a hero. You saved my life. Multiple times."

Cooper shook his head. "We saved each other," he said. "He was coming back for me—I remember that much—and you stopped him with the scissors. Otherwise, he would've gotten to the gun. You saved me."

Annabeth smiled. "Now for the second thing I need to tell you."

He could tell by her tone it was serious. Even bruised, she could read that much on his face.

Annabeth took a deep breath and said, "I won't be coming back to Rescued Paws."

"I don't under—" Cooper started.

But Annabeth didn't want to give him an opening. She needed to get this out. "Gil came to see me in the hospital a few days ago. He called in a favor and got me a phone interview with the largest accounting firm in Alaska. With his reference, I got the job and they agreed to work with me so I can go to physical therapy over the next few months. I start at the beginning of February. So, I have the next five weeks to heal and—I don't know—to get my head back in the game. It's been a rough few weeks."

"For me, too. But I never expected this."

"I know. But I need a fresh start." Annabeth snorted to herself at hearing it out loud. The irony. *Another fresh start*, she thought. Just two months after her last fresh start.

Cooper didn't speak. Annabeth watched as his face reddened. "You can't do that," he said.

"I need to," she said.

Cooper stood and started to pace in the small space. After more than a minute of pacing, muttering to himself, he stopped and faced her.

"You know," he said. "It's just as well. You quitting means I don't have to fire you."

"What?" she shot out of her chair which made her world spin and pain shoot through her arm. She held the back of the chair for support. "You weren't going to fire me."

"We have a fraternization policy at Rescued Paws. Didn't you read the manual when you started?"

"Fraternization. Really?" If he wasn't so worked up, she might have laughed.

"Yes, really. You kissed me in the snow outside Shannon's house. I simply cannot have that. It's unacceptable."

"Unacceptable? Are you kidding me? You kissed me in the

corridor. Are you going to fire yourself, too?" Annabeth was amused more than angry but she knew he was hurt.

"Don't have to because I'm firing you," he said, taking a step closer to her. "And I'm not giving you a reference. You can't expect one after only a few weeks."

"Don't need one," she said. "I already have another job."

"Well then, since you are no longer Annabeth, the Rescued Paws accountant, I have something to say to you. You, Annabeth, the person, I mean." His next step brought him closer still.

"Say it," she said.

"You know I love you, right?" He smiled. "I can finally say it now that I fired you."

"No, I didn't know that. I thought you weren't over the death of your wife. And you didn't fire me. I quit."

"No, I'm pretty sure I fired you. I'm over my wife. I certainly didn't wish her to die, but I've been over her for a long time. What I'm not over is you. I'm in love with you."

Annabeth didn't know what to say to that. Even though he was no longer her boss, her mind still told her it wasn't a good idea. Old habits die hard.

So she decided not to listen to her logical mind for once. Instead, she decided to listen to her heart. "I quit and, you know, I'm in love with you, too?"

"Yeah, I knew that."

He opened his arms and she fell into them. Gently still. Careful of his hand. Her arm, his face.

"Are you going to kiss me now?" Annabeth asked.

"No," he said. Annabeth wasn't expecting that answer. "I have a surprise for you. Come on."

He tried to hold her hand but it was awkward, since, between them, they only had two right hands. But they did it anyway, and he led her back to the lobby and then into the warehouse.

"Where are we going?" she asked.

"I told you. It's a surprise." He stopped. "Close your eyes."

"What? No."

"Come on. Close your eyes. You trust me, don't you? You have to. After all, I saved your life."

"I saved your life, too. And I quit. And I trust you." She closed her eyes.

Cooper took tiny steps and went slow. Instinct made her put her casted arm in front of her, but she desperately hoped it wouldn't bump anything because it would be terribly painful. "Almost there. Keep them closed. Okay, stop. Keep them closed," he said again.

"They're closed. Can I open them?" Annabeth asked.

"Not yet. I have a riddle for you. Well, not a riddle. You have to get the right answer to my question before you can open them."

For a moment, Annabeth thought he might be getting ready to ask her to marry him. She hoped he wouldn't. It was too soon, much too soon. "Okay," she said.

"What day is today?"

Are you kidding me? What a dumb question, she thought. "That's not a riddle. It's Friday," she said, which was too easy, she knew.

"No. Well, yes. But not the right answer. What day is today? Think," he said and squeezed her good hand.

"Okay. Let's see. It's Friday. A few days before Christmas. I have no idea. Am I close?"

She felt him lean over, felt his warm breath against the side of her face. "Starting tomorrow, the days will be getting longer," he whispered in her ear.

Then she knew.

She knew the day and, more importantly, she knew her surprise. Annabeth wished she could be the kind of person who could be dignified and graceful in moments like this. But that wasn't who she was. She started bawling. She couldn't help it. Just sobbing.

"It's the shortest day of the year. It's the winter solstice," she said and opened her eyes and fell to the ground. Cooper opened the kennel door he'd led her to. The black puppy with a white parallelogram above her right eye sprung into her lap, licking her tears, bouncing, tail swishing hard through the air. Annabeth tried to hug the squirrely ball of puppy excitement. "Solstice," Annabeth said to her. "You're saved."

It was a full 10 minutes before she stopped crying, before Solstice calmed. "Thank you," she said to Cooper as he helped her stand.

"That's not all," he said, smiling a cat-that-ate-the-canary grin.

"What else could there be?"

Cooper closed the kennel door and pointed to the paperwork on the front. Adopted was stamped in red across the top page.

"You?" she asked.

"No. You," he said. "She's been here waiting since that night, since the fifteen dogs Shannon and Jake stole were recovered."

"But. But—" Annabeth almost started to cry again. Her head swirled with emotions, her arm throbbing. "But I don't have any place for her. My apartment doesn't allow pets."

"Well, I've been thinking about your problem, thinking outside the box. And I was thinking Solstice could stay out at the cabin with me. She'd have Moose to play with. And you'd get to see her all the time."

"I would?"

"Because I'm thinking with those five weeks you have off, you could get your life in order out there. With Solstice. And with me."

"I love an orderly life," Annabeth said, smiling big at Cooper.

"I'm going to kiss you now," he said. "It's probably going to hurt my face, but I'm going to do it anyway."

"Will it be memorable?" Annabeth asked as she stepped into his arms.

"Even your toes will remember this one."

"Will it be long?"

"Hmm. That's a good question."

"What's the answer?" Annabeth asked.

"Is forever long enough for you?"

Yes, she thought, closing her eyes. *Yes, it is.*

Meet Debbie LaFleiche

After completing her MFA degree, Debbie LaFleiche went to work in Alaska's nonprofit sector where she spent most of her career as a chief financial officer. After 22 years, she quit her job, sold her house, purchased a 25-foot trailer and became a full-time RVer in search of adventure and beautiful places to park. She writes about her travel experiences here: www.SupersizeLIFE.com

Letter to Our Readers

Enjoy this book?

You can make a difference

As an independent publisher, Wings ePress, Inc. does not have the financial clout of the large New York Publishers. We can't afford large magazine spreads or subway posters to tell people about our quality books.

But, we do have something much more effective and powerful than ads. We have a large base of loyal readers.

Honest Reviews help bring the attention of new readers to our books.

If you enjoyed this book, we would appreciate it if you would spend a few minutes posting a review on the site where you purchased this book or on the Wings ePress, Inc. webpages at:
https://wingsepress.com/

Thank You

Visit Our Website

For The Full Inventory
Of Quality Books:

Wings ePress.Inc
https://wingsepress.com/

Quality trade paperbacks and downloads
in multiple formats,
in genres ranging from light romantic comedy
to general fiction and horror.
Wings has something for every reader's taste.
Visit the website, then bookmark it.
We add new titles each month!

Wings ePress Inc.
3000 N. Rock Road
Newton, KS 67114

Made in the USA
Columbia, SC
18 August 2022